The Owl That Carries Us Away

Also by Doug Ramspeck

POETRY

Original Bodies

Mechanical Fireflies

Possum Nocturne

Where We Come From

Black Tupelo Country

The Owl That Carries Us Away

STORIES

DOUG RAMSPECK

Winner of the G. S. Sharat Chandra Prize for Short Fiction
Selected by Billy Lombardo

BkMk Press
University of Missouri-Kansas City
www.umkc.edu/bkmk

BkMk Press
University of Missouri-Kansas City
5101 Rockhill Road
Kansas City, MO 64110

Executive Editor: Robert Stewart
Managing Editor: Ben Furnish
Assistant Managing Editor: Cynthia Beard

Missouri Arts Council
The State of the Arts

Financial support for BkMk Press has been provided by the Missouri Arts
Council, a state agency.

Addtional support has been provided by the Miller-Mellor Foundation.

The G. S. Sharat Chandra Prize wishes to thank Valerie Fiorivanti, Leslie
Koffler, Linda Rodriguez, and Evan Morgan Williams.

BkMk Press wishes to thank Jordan Hooper and Rachel Mills.

Library of Congress Cataloging-in-Publication Data

Names: Ramspeck, Doug, 1953- author.
Title: The owl that carries us away : short stories / by Doug Ramspeck.
Description: Kansas City, MO : BkMk Press, University of Missouri-Kansas
    City, [2017]
Identifiers: LCCN 2017045554 | ISBN 9781943491131 (acid-free paper)
Classification: LCC PS3618.A479 A6 2017 | DDC 813/.6--dc23 LC record
available at https://lccn.loc.gov/2017045554

ISBN: 978-1-943491-13-1

For Beth and Lee

Acknowledgments

Grateful acknowledgment is made to the editors of the following publications where stories in this collection were originally published:

The Antigonish Review: "Confessions of a Cloud."
Bluestem: "Three Crows."
Booth: A Journal: "The Second Coming."
Chattahoochee Review: "The Visible World."
Chautauqua: "Opuntia."
Cleaver: "Dog Memories" and "The Old Worlds."
Concho River Review: "Slippery Creek."
Confrontation: "The Green Bridge" and "The World We Know."
Cottonwood: "The Owl That Carries Us Away" and "Jamaican Snow."
December: "Folklore."
Fiction Southeast: "Crow Death."
Floyd County Moonshine: "Old Man."
Gargoyle Magazine: "Water Tower."
Green Mountains Review: "Little Dancer Aged Fourteen."
Hawai'i Pacific Review: "Baobab."
Hobart: "Bedtime Story."
The Iowa Review: "Bonjour Tristesse" and "Omphalotus Olearius."
Lake Effect: "Five Grackles."
Literary Review: "Crow."
Saranac Review: "Into the Woods."
Southwest Review: "Messenger."
Tartts Seven: "Spring Snow."
The Doctor T. J. Eckleburg Review: "Stone Garden."
Vestal Review: "Ocho Rios."
Willow Review: "Old Places."

"Messenger" was selected for a 2016 McGinnis-Ritchie Award by the editors of *Southwest Review*. "The Visible World" was reprinted in *The Orison Anthology*.

Contents

Foreword

In this dream I used to have when I was a kid, a great gray cloud pressed down on me like a silent scream. I don't know how else to explain it.

I think, though, that Doug Ramspeck, the author of *The Owl That Carries Us Away,* was haunted by the same dream, and these twenty-nine stories represent his attempt to wake up from it.

I don't think poetry can do what Ramspeck does here with story. Men and women stand at windows tormented with secrets, with memory, wanting, absence, loss. Ramspeck creates a silence so thick, you flinch to hear dialogue. What isn't silent, is snow-muffled, and what snow there is, is blood-spotted.

The *Now* in *The Owl That Carries Us Away* seems to exist only for the purpose of urging forth memory. And if there is happiness and hope anywhere, they are only in the *Then.*

These are the stories a poet can't tell in poems, but there is poetry here, too. Doug Ramspeck has given us something to remember.

Billy Lombardo

The Owl That Carries Us Away

The boy is washing the possum skull with his mother's hose. He found it in the mud beside the river. It was half-buried and stubborn, even when he poked it with a stick, even when he tried to pry it free with his fingers. Now he cleans the dirt out of the sockets with the spray of the hose. Pours the water through the teeth. Watches the water sliding across the pale bone. Hears the water splashing against the stone steps. The light snow that is falling is bone colored, too, as though the great skeleton of sky has broken into shards and is coming down, falling out of the fat and low-slung clouds, and the boy carries the skull through the kitchen door, hiding it behind his back. Something is frying on the stove, lifting smoke, sizzling a complaint, but his mother isn't there to tend to it. The room has been left by itself, the glasses and plates abandoned on the kitchen table. The boy hurries through the kitchen and up the narrow stairs with the skull. The stairway in the ancient house—built shortly after the Civil War—reminds him in its narrowness of the dark passage of a cave. He enters his bedroom and closes the door behind him. He lies on his bed and holds the skull on his chest. Strokes his hand across the hard, smooth bone. Feels for ridges and bumps and openings and crevices. Thinks of a cat purring beneath the rhythm of a palm. He pets the skull until he hears his mother calling out, and then he pushes it under the bed, far back in the darkness.

"Wait here," he says.

At dinner the boy sneaks looks at his father while he is eating. His father's hair is starting to grow back, but the boy can still see strange patterns and odd lines beneath the thin strands. The scars are puckered and pinkish on the white skin. Sometimes they seem to trail off like snakes. Other times they look like railroad tracks. When the bandages first came off, the boy was reminded of a swollen pumpkin, of something that only vaguely resembled the father he had known. His father stabs at his meat with his fork and cuts off a small piece with his knife. The pork chop looks slippery on his plate. He gets a small piece loose and lifts it to his mouth. Chews. The exertion of the chewing leaves him breathless. The scars shift from pink to a deeper red. He puts down his knife and fork and leans back in his chair, leaving most of the food untouched on his plate. He leans back in his chair and says something, but his voice is garbled. The words sound like they are spoken through rocks. The boy sips his milk and looks out the window at the snow coming down.

"Look at that, you two," his mother says. "It's snowing."

The boy imagines the possum waddling at some point down by the river. Its bald, long tail. Its moon-white face. The possum dying by the river, then shedding its body until all that was left in the mud was its skull.

THERE IS A LIMESTONE house on the bus ride to school, a house with a chain-link fence around the front yard. There is an American flag on a white pole. There is a small German shepherd that runs back and forth along the line of the fence as soon as it sees the bus. The dog barks and runs, runs and barks. The boy sees Biggs waiting just outside the fence, his hands in his pockets. He isn't wearing a hat, and his hair is being blown this way and that in the wind. The flag is being blown this way and that, too. The dog is still running along the fence line. The bus brakes squeak. The barking of the dog sounds louder when the bus doors whoosh open and Biggs climbs on board and walks down the aisle. The smell of the refinery enters the bus with

Biggs, follows him. Biggs sits next to the boy and punches him hard on the arm near the shoulder.

"Asshole," he says.

The next hit lands in almost exactly the same spot, and the next one after that does as well.

"Look at how stupid skinny you are," Biggs says. "I bet I weigh twice what you do."

The fist comes down hard again on the boy's shoulder. The side of a hard shoe kicks his leg. Biggs moves closer and presses the boy against the window, holding him pinned. It's like the weight of the bus itself.

The boy looks out the window. They are stopping before a house that backs up to the Johnson River. The muddy waters of the river are flowing, except near the shore where there are small patches of ice shimmering brightly in the morning sunlight. The ice looks like strange tumbled jewels. This is the same river that goes past the boy's own backyard, out in the woods. In the summers he sees muskrats swimming in its shallows. He throws rocks at them. Sometimes he goes swimming in the river. There are supposed to be leeches that will clutch to your skin and won't come off unless you burn them. They suck your blood and grow fat as a finger on your body.

"I hear your Dad talks like a retard," Biggs says.

The boy doesn't answer.

"Walks like he's drunk," Biggs says. "Like he's a spaz." Biggs hits him once more while pressing his body hard against him. Biggs smells like something dying at the deep back of a dark cave. He says, "I hear he couldn't even do the job right. How can you miss from that close up? You touch your head and pull the trigger."

"Shut up," the boy says.

The brakes squeal again as the bus comes to a stop in the school parking lot. Everybody stands. Everybody walks toward the door, filing out into the cold air. The boy can see his breath escaping from his mouth like a cloud or a strange spirit. Biggs keeps bumping against him, sticking out a foot to try to trip him, pressing his knuckles into the small of his back, whispering names against his neck. Soon the boy is free of the bus and hurries toward the door. They aren't allowed to run, but he walks as fast as he can, weaving in and out of the other students. He steps inside the building and hears his shoes clapping loudly on the shiny floor. The old janitor is standing on a ladder, changing a light bulb. The old janitor looks at him and seems unsteady on the ladder, like he might at any moment fall. The light bulb is sputtering. It sounds like a voice. The boy hurries toward the safety of the classroom.

IN THE BOY'S DREAM an owl is flying out of the gray-orange sky. At first the owl appears to be part of an upper limb of a hickory tree, made of bark and wood, but then it comes to life. It flies above the river and holds in its talons a possum skull. Or maybe it is holding in its talons a living possum. The possum squirms but can't loosen the owl's grip. On the ground the boy runs through the woods and tries to keep the owl in sight. He crosses the river, swimming, and then he runs into an open field he's never seen before. The field is tall with corn in the dead of winter, and the boy runs through the tall stalks that are frozen like upright icicles. The owl moves slowly by flapping its great wings, and the boy is powerless to keep up, but still he runs until he reaches the railroad tracks. There are turkey vultures on the tracks, which confuse the boy, for he was certain he saw the owl land there and begin feeding on the possum. The vultures are eating the dead flesh, and then the boy feels the talons of the owl lift him by his own flesh, the flesh of his back, and he is being carried away from the ground, away from any life as he has known it. Higher and higher he moves into the air, until the house where he lives with his father and his mother is a small speck on the ground, and the school where he spends his days is a small speck, and he knows his back should be hurting from the talons but it's not, and he wonders if he's become a skull as he's being carried, if that is all anyone would see from the ground.

He comes awake and climbs from bed. He grabs the skull from its hiding place and carries it with him back under the covers. He places the skull on his chest, aiming it forward, and he strokes the smooth bone with his palm. Some nights he falls asleep like this. And he knows that when his mother comes into his room in the morning, he will quickly hide the skull beneath the blankets. When his mother is gone, he will touch his lips to the skull. The bone will feel cool against his lips. The empty eyes will look up at him. He will rock the skull in his arms like an infant. He will think about the skull while he's at school. He will imagine it hiding all day beneath the bed, its eyes glowing the way you see raccoon eyes glowing green in the woods in the summer. He will imagine the skull waiting for him to return. Imagine the skull feeling lonely beneath the bed and listening for his footsteps on the stairs, holding its breath, waiting for the bedroom door to come open and admit him.

IT IS SATURDAY. THE boy is holding his mother's gardening trowel in his hand. The boy is digging. Digging in the mud by the river. The ground is cold and hard. The boy is wearing gloves, but still his fingers are numb. Each time he lifts more earth, each time he wedges more dirt loose and throws it in a small pile by the river, he looks through the pile for bones. He imagines the bones will be in the dirt like worms. He imagines finding the rest of the possum, bone by bone. He figures that a possum, even a dead one, can't have a head without a body. The body is waiting in the ground, if only he can find it. He imagines placing that body in a box beneath his bed, placing the skull atop the box.

When it is lunch time and his mother calls out from the back of the house, he gives up digging. His mother has made grilled-cheese sandwiches. Some of the cheese has dripped over the sides and has burned into the bread. There are potato chips and carrot sticks. The sticks make a crunching sound as he chews them. He closes his eyes for a moment and imagines he is crunching down on bones. His mother stands over the table while he is eating. She says, "Your friend's mom called."

"What?"

"She said you're his only friend. It's sad, really."

"What are you talking about?"

"Her name is Dorothy. She sounded very nice on the phone. He's coming over."

"Who?"

"Your friend from school. The mom called to set up the play date."

"Who are you talking about?"

When Biggs arrives, they go out in the woods together. The mothers remain behind, talking on the driveway. Biggs is wearing a baseball cap and winter boots. He makes large footprints in the snow. The boy shows Biggs the river, which is frozen with a thin skin of ice you can break through if you stamp on it or throw a heavy enough log or rock. For a time they have races with dead leaves in the open patches of water they've created. They have stick-throwing contests, seeing who can hit certain trees on the far side of the river. Biggs throws hard but not straight. Later they throw rocks at squirrels, but the squirrels are high up in the trees. The boy has a BB gun his mother locked in the blue trunk in the garage. This was the same time she got rid of his father's guns. Gave them to the police to get rid of. The blue trunk has a padlock, but the boy knows the key is in the coffee can on the shelf by the toolbox. They carry the BB gun into the woods and take turns shooting. Biggs shoots at the squirrels but doesn't hit any. The boy shoots at a bluejay. The bird flies off. Finally Biggs hits a junco that looks puffed up and frozen on an oak limb in the cold. The junco falls to the ground but is still squirming. Biggs shoots it from close range. The gray wings are still flapping. Biggs gives the gun to the boy to take a shot. He touches the barrel almost to the white belly and pulls the trigger. There is blood in the snow. They take turns shooting until the junco is lying still and its dark eyes are blank. They lift the bird by the feathers and throw it in the muddy river. It floats, and they take turns shooting while the current carries it downstream. They watch the bird snag where the ice starts up again, and they shoot it seven or eight more times.

When they get back to the house, they take off their muddy shoes before going inside. The boy's mother, who called out to the woods earlier to tell them she was going to the drugstore, has left some cookies on the kitchen table. They are Oreos. They eat the Oreos and pour themselves some apple juice. They get the package of Oreos out of the kitchen cabinet and pour more cookies onto the table in a pile.

Biggs says, "Let me see him."

"See who?"

"Your father."

"Why?"

"I want to."

They walk together down the hallway to the Florida Room. The boy doesn't know why it's called that. As far as he knows, no one in his family has ever been to Florida. The room uses a space heater for warmth. It glows, especially in the dark. In the dark it looks like something inside it is on fire. But it isn't dark now. There's a big stuffed dead fish over the couch. In the past the boy has climbed on the couch and run his hands over the fish. He has put his fingers in the mouth of the fish to feel where its teeth should be. He has run his fingers over the hardened fins and tail. His father is lying on the couch with his eyes closed. Music is playing from the radio. It is music without words. You can wait for the words but they don't ever come. The boy takes Biggs to the entrance of the room and lets him peek in. His father has a blanket up to his armpits, and open pages of the newspaper are lying on the floor by the couch. Some of them are crumpled. There's a plate on the TV tray beside the couch, and on that plate are the remains of a grilled cheese sandwich. The boy leans against the bookshelf and lets Biggs stare at his father. His father's hair hasn't grown back yet, and the scars are visible through the winter light falling through the tall windows. His father is snoring a little, or maybe breathing loudly, but it's hard to hear over the sound of the music without words. There are violins or something, and they are very loud. Biggs stands there for a long time, but then he turns and walks out. They go up the stairs to the boy's room and sit on his bed.

Biggs lies back on the bed and puts his hands behind his head. "It must have hurt," he says. "It must have hurt like hell."

The boy rises from the bed and walks over to the window. He wishes it would snow again. He likes to watch the snow falling out of the sky, falling down from the clouds on their long journey, falling like strange moths.

"Why did he do it?" Biggs asks.

The boy says, "I'll show you something if you promise not to tell anyone."

"What?"

The boy gets down on his knees and reaches under the bed. He pulls out the skull and holds it atop his two palms. Biggs reaches out and takes it from the boy. He turns it in his hands. He runs his fingers over the sharp rows of teeth. He sticks his fingers in the eye sockets.

"What is it?" Biggs asks.

"Possum."

"Can I take it?"

"No."

"Just to borrow."

"My mother will see it. She'll take it from us."

"We'll hide it in something."

"No. You can't have it."

When Biggs leaves to go home with his mother, he is carrying a plastic bag. The boy watches the bag as Biggs carries it toward the green car. He watches the green car drive off with the bag and with Biggs. He sees Biggs sitting in the front seat. He sees the car round the corner at Wallace Street. Then he can't see the car at all.

THE BOY'S FATHER IS bleeding. He is bleeding in his head. That's what they say. The doctors. They don't know why. The boy's mother is crying a lot. She is crying right now in the waiting room. The father is back in the hospital. The hospital smells. They are cutting into his head with a knife to make the bleeding stop. It doesn't make sense. The boy wants to ask his mother how a knife can stop bleeding, but his mother doesn't seem to want to talk. They have been sitting in the waiting room for a long time. It is boring. There is another family in that same waiting room, including a baby dressed in a yellow one-piece, and the baby keeps crying and then spitting out its pacifier. The mother puts the pacifier back in, but then the baby starts to cry again and it falls out on the carpet. The carpet is blue-green. Later the boy's uncle shows up, and the boy hears him talking to his mother, and he hears his mother saying how bad things are. Everything is taking a very long time. When the boy has to go the bathroom, his uncle walks him down the hallway. Later the boy sees his father briefly, though his eyes are closed, and there are bandages on his head like the ones he had last time, bandages where the knife probably went in to make the bleeding stop.

By the next evening the boy is able to sit on the edge of the bed with his father, who speaks in a soft, roughened voice that is impossible to understand, but mostly his father wants to sleep. Outside the hospital window there is a parking lot and then a small outdoor ice-skating rink, and the boy stands at the window and watches the people skating. He sees a little girl with a pink stocking cap fall down. There are bright lights that make it easy to watch. The boy watches the same girl to see if she'll fall down again. He wants her to.

A few days later his father comes home, though he isn't as strong as he was and his hair is shaved off again. There are a few bits of hair here and there, but that's it. The boy sees that there are new scars, new stitches. He is supposed to be quiet in the house, though he keeps forgetting. His father can't stand up now without help.

THIS TIME WHEN BIGGS comes over it is snowing and they go sledding at the reservoir. Afterward they drink hot cocoa with a floating marshmallow. Biggs asks to shoot the BB gun again, and they do. Later he explains that he forgot to bring the skull. It was an honest mistake. He says he'll have his mother arrange to play at his house the next day after church.

So his mother drives the boy over on Sunday afternoon following lunch. It's the limestone house with the fence and the flag and the dog. The dog growls and the boy doesn't want to go through the gate, but Biggs yells at the dog and it runs off, though not very far. It growls from the side of the house but doesn't come any closer. Biggs and the boy go out to the road, hide behind a hedge, throw rocks at passing cars, and run. They throw rocks at the neighbor's shed. They lob rocks over the fence at the dog, which growls and runs when the rocks land. Later they go into Biggs' room, turn on the TV, and lie on the floor.

"Where is it?" the boy asks.

"What?"

"The skull."

"In my closet."

"Get it out."

"After the show."

The boy goes over to the closet and opens the accordion doors. It smells like cedar. The clothes are packed tightly on the hangers. There are dirty white socks in a pile. There is a baseball catcher's mitt. There is a cowboy belt with a large shiny buckle, hanging from a hook.

"What are you doing?" Biggs says.

"Getting the skull."

Biggs grabs him by the arm and they wrestle. The boy throws a punch into Biggs' fat belly, but nothing comes of it. He tries to push Biggs away from the closet, but it is like trying to push a brick wall. Outside, the dog is barking at something, and there are sounds of gunfire on the television. Then there are sounds of cars chasing each other. By this time Biggs is sitting on top of him. The carpeting smells like dirty feet. The boy's face is pressed into the carpet. His arm is under him in a way that twists it and makes it hurt. A house has fallen on him. His ribs hurt, and he can't breathe.

"You're not ever getting it back," Biggs says.

IT IS MORNING. THEY are on the bus. Biggs is punching him on the arm. The boy is ignoring it. Biggs hits him harder, but still the boy keeps looking out the window. Biggs is asking if he can come over after school, maybe get off the bus at his house, but the boy says no. Biggs is asking if he wants to spend the night over the weekend. He says he's cleared it with his mother. The boy says no.

"Why?" Biggs asks.

On Thursday Biggs tells him his father has some leftover fireworks, and if he comes over on Saturday, they can set them off. Once again he brings up the idea about spending the night—maybe they can even go bowling. The boy is looking out the bus window. The boy imagines himself as still as stone, as still as a statue. Not one word comes out of his mouth.

On Saturday morning Biggs' mother phones the boy's mother, but he has already told her no, never. He goes out in the woods by himself, and he walks down to the river, which has melted a little and is flowing so quickly now he can hear it. It makes a sound like something garbled in a throat. The boy wants to see how cold the water feels, so he takes off his shoes and socks and walks into it. The water is so cold it feels like it's burning. When the boy comes out of the water, his feet and his ankles are pink. He puts his socks and shoes back on. Later Biggs phones him, but the boy hangs up the moment he recognizes the voice. He slams the phone down, and his father looks up from the kitchen table but doesn't say anything. The boy goes up to his room and finds some matches he has hidden in with some playing cards. He takes the matches out to the river, lights them one by one, and throws them into the muddy water. He likes to hear the sound of them being extinguished. He likes the smell of the sulfur.

On Monday Biggs gets on the bus as usual, but this time he is carrying a plastic bag. He sits down next to the boy but doesn't speak. He is breathing heavily. He is wearing his baseball cap. He unzips his coat and stamps his boots on the floor of the bus to get the snow off. Slush falls from his boots and starts to melt on the black rubber padding on the bus floor. He holds the plastic bag in his lap as the bus doors whoosh closed and the bus starts down the road toward the school. The bus sways a little, especially when they go over the railroad tracks. Biggs and the boy bump against each other. Finally Biggs takes the plastic bag from his lap and hands it to the boy. The boy lets the bag sit there for a moment, untouched, but then he lifts it and looks inside. Even the teeth are broken into pieces. The skull has been smashed. It's a plastic bag full of bone dust, bone slivers, bone shards, bone chunks. Biggs must have taken a hammer to it. He must have taken a hammer for an hour to be that thorough. The boy reaches into the bag and feels the remains of the skull. Some of the bone bits are sharp and jab against his fingers. He hears those bone pieces bumping against each other as the bus jiggles. The boy closes the bag and starts to speak, but something unexpected happens. He can't believe it at first, can't accept it, even though there's no doubt that it is true. Everyone on the bus is turning to look at him. This is the most humiliating moment of his life. He knows he will never hear the end of it, that he will be known forever as the boy who did this, but he can't stop. His chest is convulsing. His shoulders are convulsing. He is crying. Not just a little but weeping openly, the tears pouring from his eyes, the wails escaping in throttled moans from his strangled throat. Even his nose is running. The tears won't stop. And now he doesn't think they ever will.

The Visible World

I used to think you might carry the past willingly on your shoulders, ferry it through the years, until you grew so accustomed to its presence it would no longer have the capacity to wound you. It would become, instead, as familiar yet distant from your daily preoccupations as the bones inside your body.

Today it is Saturday, in late June, and my wife is asleep not ten feet from where I am standing at this window. Her breaths are a small passage. Her hair, crow black, has composed itself across the pillow, the knobs of her backbone visible from between where the sheet leaves off and her red T-shirt has climbed nearly as high as her first ribs.

Outside the window our two boys are playing beneath the gray Ohio sky. The yard is barely visible around them. They are up early, as usual, out by the barn. Watching them, I wonder if it is possible to slice away all the complications of a life, all the context and histories and personal fabrications. Perhaps I am no longer a small-town lawyer living on a pretend farm on which my only real crop is an abundance of weeds, and my wife is not a fourth-grade teacher and photographer, and my boys are not Sammy and Jackson, nine and eight, but simply two voices outside a window.

One of the voices that drew me from bed is agitated, angry. It is Jackson yelling at his older brother to *stop stop stop*. Now, as I watch, I see that my sons are wild creatures, feral boys in the backyard, one half-hiding behind a great white oak, the other half-hiding behind a decaying wall of the barn. They are throwing dirt balls or maybe even stones, the primitive missiles cutting through the dull air. I visualize the fierce trajectory of a conjured stone, a slow-motion strike, the blood on the towel I hold against my son's eye while helping him to the car so I can drive him with frantic agitation to the hospital.

If my wife were standing here beside me, I know, she would bend down to the screen mesh and cast her voice like her own hard stone into the morning. Our boys, sheepish, would bow their heads or maybe shrug or roll their eyes, but in any case they would desist, drop whatever weaponry they were clutching, and slump back inside to switch on the television to their cartoons.

But my own voice is marooned inside me, becalmed, and I know why. My thoughts have tumbled back to where they always go. Is it possible to worry the same few minutes of a life over and over the way you keep touching a tongue tip to an aching tooth? My mind has learned the route by rote, travels here without any prompting or delay.

I am boy again myself, a year older than my older son is now. And my own brother, Daniel, is two years older than I am. It is winter, which means we are at the mercy of snow that knows only to fall from the sky and try to smother everything. We are living in Escanaba, Michigan, with a view from the back of the house of the Wallace River. I know that memory is forever a form of interpretation, as malleable as any tall tale, but still I feel as though the years have slipped away, and I am back on that December morning over the Christmas holiday, back with Danny at the river's verge, the frozen river motionless before us, stilled in time. And we are walking onto it, this stopped current that, in summer, carries us downstream when we go swimming, the mud waters leaving us without volition. We give ourselves over, which is what it means, I sometimes think, to be alive.

In memory, though, there is one moment that feels like a kind of permanence. The ash clouds are low-slung above us, and we are treading carefully onto the thin skin of ice and snow. The surface creaks beneath us, faintly buckling, and then my brother disappears from view, as suddenly as that, and there is a dark hole in the ice where a moment earlier there was pure white, and a silver sheen beneath it. I think, looking back, of the blown pupil of an eye. And it is silent on the river, as silent as a held breath. Danny isn't waving his arms or shouting or splashing. There is simply this cavernous hole in the fabric of the world. My brother belongs, now, to the geography beyond sight, which, as far as we know, isn't actually any geography at all. And I am standing there, standing. I am not moving toward the opening to find him. I am not racing back to the house to tell my mother or my father. I am not shouting *help help*. There is just the soundlessness of the snow coming down, the faint feathering of my own breaths. Looking back, I can easily see the police and ambulance when they finally arrive, can easily see myself standing before my brother's grave, can easily imagine the weight of the years when I think of Danny like the distant sound of a train whistle that never seems to come any closer, can easily see myself rising in the morning to spy my own sons throwing rocks at each other and shouting, my wife's figure quiet in bed. But none of that is real, of course. It never has been. All that is real is the ice beneath my feet, the snow coming down, and the black opening of river.

Omphalotus Olearius

She sees it from the window while her new husband is still sleeping. That is how she thinks of him: *her new husband*. As though he is still shiny, just off the store shelf. They have known each other, now, for almost a year, but they've been married for less than a month, living together these few short weeks. It's an adjustment. She moved from her apartment near the center of Decatur to his trailer on the outskirts of town. She is reminded of bathrooms like upright coffins on buses or airplanes—but there are two of them in this one, two of them navigating the same narrow space. *Which makes our love only more intense,* she likes to think. She is working as a waitress while he is working as a roofer and an occasional carpenter. Money is tight. But they are happy. They have their bodies, after all, which grow hungry in the narrow space of the trailer. He arrives home from work, slick with sweat, his shoulders and neck and face fevered red from the sun, and they fall upon each other. What more could anyone want? Eventually they will have children, of course, and eventually they will build a life beyond this bed where they sleep, by necessity, in each other's arms. But for now, she imagines that their orgasms on that bed are like spirits or ghosts lifting to fill the air in the trailer all around them, to reverberate and echo. And she is thinking about these pleasures when she rises in the night to use the toilet, when she sees out the tiny window a blue-green glow perhaps ten yards from the trailer. It appears alive in pale light not far from where her husband's pickup is parked. She gazes, perplexed. The light appears to live at the foot of a tree, the wraith of it trailing out across the ground. And not until morning does she realize it was mushrooms she was seeing, jack-o'-lanterns that, by day, appear yellowish-orange. They are growing wild from the earth, multiplying. They appear disfigured, somehow, like hideous flowers, dead growths that rise into the air. She finds the sight of them unsettling, disturbing, and thoughts of them keep returning to her mind during her lunch shift at work. She is so distracted that she drops an order of wings with barbecue sauce into the lap of one of her favorite customers. She is so distracted that she doesn't see a squirrel until the final moment as she is driving home. Through the rearview mirror she watches the creature rolling toward the bar ditch, then lying still. The tail is twitching, but the rest of the squirrel has already died. At home she showers, then walks outside again to stare at the mushrooms. There is a smell to them—she can't decide if it is pleasant or disgusting. All she knows for certain is that the growths remind her of something decaying, something fetid, vile. She finds a shovel in the tiny locked shed at the side of the trailer, then chops at the heads of the mushrooms, destroying them. But when she is making love that evening with her husband, she notices on his shoulder a small patch of discolored skin, the same orange-yellow hue as those mushrooms. It disturbs her. There is a smell to her husband, as well, like stagnant waters. She loves him, of course, loves what he makes her feel with his body, but still she keeps gazing at his shoulder while he is thrusting, keeps studying the skin that doesn't remind her of skin at all but something unsightly, inhuman. And that night she dreams that he is standing shirtless in their miniscule kitchen, and she notices that mushrooms are growing on his back and chest and arms. They are jack-o'-lanterns, though she also notices on his legs—he is wearing shorts—what appear to be clusters of hen-of-the-woods. She is horrified by the sight, and yet he presses toward her, trying to smother her with his body. Some of the mushrooms fall to the floor and turn black and wilt before her eyes. She awakes breathing heavily. She goes into the bathroom and looks out the window, seeing the glow of more of those mushrooms, or perhaps the same ones she decapitated. The glow seems to be whispering, laughing. In the morning her husband kisses her before he leaves for his job—it is always barely light out when he rises—and his breath is something decaying in the woods. And when that evening they go for a walk around their trailer park—they like to hike down to Lost Creek—she notices how primitive he seems beside her, as wild and feral as those mushrooms. She begins to wonder what drew her to him in the first place, why she believed it made sense that they might marry. A week passes like that. Another. She wants desperately to love him, wants to accept his body when he forces himself atop her, but she keeps thinking of those mushrooms: how they gather on the earth around the trailer. She can sense them growing there, sense them springing from the mud of the ground, springing from dead wood. Her mother used to warn her about the poison of mushrooms, how you could die from consuming them, and she imagines the mushrooms growing so thick around her that they swallow her, swallow the trailer. She can't imagine living like this much longer. From her old apartment in town, her window looked out on the YMCA. She misses that. Misses being alone inside the walls. Her husband wasn't always coming at her with his body, clinging the way mushrooms cling to the earth, staining it. But still she fears she has accepted this, will soon find the mushrooms springing up in her dreams from the soft skin behind her knees, there where the legs bend, or flourishing in the moist cave of her mouth, deep beneath her tongue.

Stone Garden

There was a picture book Cole liked that told the story of a mother who had a child with accordion-like wings on his shoulders, tiny wings that would carry him into the air if his mother wasn't careful, sometimes bumping against ceilings or tree branches or clouds. It wasn't clear to Rachel how much her nephew understood about the story, but he sat in her lap on the bus while she was reading it, touching his little fingers to the page, making sounds that might or might not have been words. Rachel had been terrified of getting caught earlier when she had bundled little Cole in a blanket at her sister's home, had carried him from the house while the parents were asleep, had walked the half mile to the bus stop. She had worried that, at a minimum, the boy would start fussing for his mother, but it hadn't happened. He was a beautiful child, everything she'd always hoped for. He was small as a miracle, a perfect child with pudgy legs and cute pudgy cheeks and his first tiny teeth fighting through.

On the bus, they rode past small towns with names like Vermillion, Newcomb, Mansfield, Olney, and Pennville. She sang quietly to Cole, songs she remembered from childhood. It was snowing by the middle of the day, the desultory flakes drifting out of the sky without conviction, falling against the window and then evaporating. Much later the bus passed over the Tennessee River. It was a gray river, much larger than she'd expected, a great expanse of living liquid, the current moving on a treadmill or a factory line. Cole began squirming more in her arms, but eventually they both slept, and when she came awake it was the first gray of morning, and the land had flattened out. There were trees by the side of the road she'd never seen before, and the color of the grass—if it was grass—was new to her as well. She sat up in the seat and tried to picture finding a waitressing job, walking home at the end of her shift, unlocking the apartment door with her key, handing the babysitter a few dollars, finding Cole playing on the floor and grinning wildly to see her, waving his little arms for her to lift him. It was a perfect dream, and she held him close to her body when at last they arrived at Pensacola, when she climbed off the bus. It wasn't as warm as she'd expected. A brisk wind was blowing.

There were supposed to be white beaches by the Pensacola Bay, supposed to be a beautiful view of the Gulf of Mexico, but all she saw so far were a few dirty streets. She walked them, stopping often to shift the suitcase and Cole into opposite arms. The air smelled different than back home: she realized it was the bay she was smelling, the ocean. It wasn't a salt smell but more like old fish and cresting waves. She checked into a cheap motel called The Bayview, paying cash and signing a false name. She fed Cole mashed bananas and strained vegetables out of a jar. She unwrapped a little blue pacifier. He had a mild case of diaper rash but not bad. The television wasn't showing any cartoons, but she did find a show where two young women were singing, and Cole slapped his little hands on the carpet and seemed happy enough. Later she carried Cole down to the beach—if that was what it was. There wasn't any sand, just the majestic waters of the bay stretching out like a great slab of dark marble or stone. She could see the Pensacola Bay Bridge reaching like a straight finger across the water, and she could see the hazy slab of land where the road was headed. There were water birds flying everywhere around the bay, but not one with a name she knew. She sat on a bench and bounced Cole in her lap. She breathed in the air and tried not to think about her sister, who'd once gone to California and had said that swimming in the ocean was like being swallowed by a great liquid beast that was heaven. She was still thinking about her sister when she fell asleep that night and dreamed that it was snowing. She was walking past an outdoor fountain, and in the shallows of the moving water there were stone alligators and stone frogs and even a stone mermaid with naked and unusually pronounced breasts. It was Rachel's birthday in the dream: she was forty. Above her the clouds were low-slung and the color of stone, but mostly her eyes were on the fountain. Beneath the surface there were stonefish muscling through the reeds. They might have been alive or they might have been mechanical. Then she woke and kissed a sleeping Cole on his forehead.

Two more days passed like that: she spent each one with Cole at the water's edge, having little picnics with him in the sand. There was a gift shop near the pier, and she splurged on a postcard that showed the very same view she'd been staring at all day. She walked to the end of the pier and put down Cole on the weathered wood and sat with him and watched the sun sinking lower in the sky. A few sea birds went flying past. For supper she and Cole went to a restaurant for the first time since they'd arrived in Florida, spending the last of the money she'd brought with her. She ordered more than they could eat and dessert, too. Cole was a little fussy but it passed. Afterward, she carried him back to the ocean so they could see the sun coming down, sinking like a great flame being doused in the gulf to the west. She thought of the sound that a hot frying pan makes when it is placed into a sink of water, but the sun slipped soundlessly into the ocean, then was gone. There was a pay phone she'd passed on the corner beyond the pier, and she found it and called collect. Cole was squirming in her arms, so she put him down and let him play by her feet. There were cars going by on the road, people walking by on the sidewalks, as though it were an ordinary night, as though it were no different than any other, as though life would go on like this and never stop. She listened to the phone ringing. It rang four times then her sister answered. "It's me," Rachel said. "I'm so sorry. Cole's okay." Then both she and her sister were crying, and Bev was talking very fast in a loud, angry voice, telling her that she was going to go to prison, so

Rachel hung up and lifted the boy in her arms. He was heavy—in a good way. She stopped so they could look one last time at the ocean, then carried him down the street until she saw the building with tan bricks. She had passed it before, had made a wide berth. She went inside and saw fluorescent lights and dark carpeting and a police officer standing behind a desk with a phone against his ear. She walked toward him and scooted Cole's butt up on the counter. The police officer was talking loudly into the phone and put up one finger to let her know he'd been done soon. She waited. The man had a mustache. There were maybe a half dozen people in the room, most sitting and waiting, though Rachel couldn't have guessed for what. She poked Cole lightly in the belly while they were waiting—a little game they liked to play. She grabbed his little legs in both hands and moved them back and forth like he was running. Cole started grinning. He had little dimples she loved. He started pumping his little legs on his own. The police officer put down the phone. "What can I help you with?" he asked.

Bonjour Tristesse

The first time she began reading the thin little paperback, she was fifteen and lying naked on a narrow bed upstairs from the bookstore on Wilmare Avenue. The book was written by a French author, Françoise Sagan, who was only eighteen when it appeared. The main character, Cécile, was seventeen. There was a quote from Oscar Wilde in the book that the main character claimed she hoped to live by: "Sin is the only note of vivid colour that persists in the modern world." Clearly it was wonderfully adult, wicked, and romantic to be reading about Cécile and her summer with her father and his mistress on the French Riviera while she herself was in the nude, and Calvin—he was thirty-four—was crouched at his desk and working with a pencil and paper on a novel of his own. He'd read her passages from it that were terminally descriptive and dull, but that wasn't the point. It was Thursday and her parents believed she was staying after school for Debate Club. She had arrived at the bookstore earlier, the bells tinkling above her head as she came through the door, had seen Calvin there behind the desk, sitting not before a cash register but before what always reminded her of the sort of tackle box her father used for fishing. She loved Calvin, of course. It ached how much she loved him, how often she thought about his life at the bookstore, about his body, how glad she was that they were lovers. Always when she arrived, he would wait for any lingering customers to leave, would turn the sign on the door to "Closed," would lead her past the rope and up the stairs to the rooms where he lived, would undress her and push her back on the bed, telling her they shouldn't be doing this, she was too young, but she was beautiful, beautiful. She thought about him often while listening to her teachers blathering on at school, while talking to her classmates and friends. She felt older now than all of them, as old as the moon, as old as the snow coming down. She'd first begun sleeping with Calvin in October, and now, in January, she had begun to dream they would keep up their secret affair until she was eighteen. Then they would marry and move to France where Calvin would be a famous novelist, and she would be his muse. Or maybe she would begin to write herself, the beauty of her creations eclipsing even Calvin's success, and he would be jealous and storm out, vowing never to return. But he would come back at once, of course, going down on his knees to press his face against her belly or maybe lower, to beg her forgiveness, to tell her it was embarrassing to admit, the worst display of sentimental emotion, but he couldn't bear to exist without her. Which is not to say that everything was perfect between them in the bookstore. It was boring sometimes, if truth be told. She enjoyed the rush of emotions when Calvin insisted they couldn't keep seeing each other this way, that it was wrong, wrong, that he was taking advantage, that he was far too old. And she loved the way he seemed to worship at the altar of her body. But too often it was just Calvin writing at his desk while she was reading, Calvin offering her coffee and telling her how impossible the bookstore business was, how broke he was, how slowly his novel was going, that publishers didn't want novels anymore in any case, that the entire publishing business was dying. She wanted to go out somewhere, wanted to sit with him at a restaurant or even at a bar, but always he refused. People wouldn't understand, he said. And they wouldn't, of course, but wasn't that the point? They would bear the shame of the looks from others—or defiantly move past them. Sometimes they also argued about love. Calvin kept saying that it couldn't last between them, shouldn't last, but she kept insisting they would stay together forever. And he did love her, she knew. He wrote her love letters that included lines about how much he wanted her, how much he desired her body. And he drew a sketch of them naked together. She hadn't known, before then, that he was an artist as well as a novelist. It was tragic what they had between them, so it hurt her when she broke it off in May, told him she wouldn't be coming back, that if he saw her again it would only be to ask him for advice about books to read. The entire time she'd known him, after all, he had always pressed books into her hands, including the Françoise Sagan novels, and *Confessions of a Mask* by Yukio Mishima, and Dostoyevsky's *Notes from Underground.* She had read them all, but now she'd met a boy in her class named Wade Stevenson, a senior, who seemed actually more worldly than Calvin—he'd lived on an army base in Germany as a child—less trapped in a stuffy bookstore and complaining about paying the mortgage. She still loved Calvin, though, would always love him, and from time to time she returned to his bookstore to glance through the dusty rows of books, to pick one or two or three novels, to carry them over to Calvin and his tackle box, to watch the look in his eyes while he told her they were free, to take them.

Messenger

H ere is the place, as quiet as a whisper. It is old here at the far edge of the woods where the fence lies down. It has fallen mostly in one spot, where the brothers cross on their way into the open field and school. Their footsteps swoosh through undergrowth conjured from the fetid earth, the boys walking this way instead of passing through the neighborhood with arcing sprinklers and barking, hidden dogs and watchful eyes. It is a ritual for them. They head out from the house, their lunch boxes in their hands. And they never take the bus, though school has resumed after the dense and muggy summer, and the boys hear the buses lumbering in the distance like great beasts along the streets, swallowing children into their interiors.

The place where the brothers walk keeps its own council. There is the smell here of loam and decaying leaves. And, in summer, there were wildflowers with names the boys don't know or want to know. A flower has its body for a brief time, then fades, which makes it beyond the world of names. And the small geography at the back of the woods is contemplative in the shade when the sunlight angles through the trees or across the field, when rain falls or insects lift themselves from the swales, swarming.

But mostly there is the creek, no more wide in places than the length of a child's body, though the burrow of it carves deep into the mud. It is here where the brothers studied over the vast sea of summer—mostly at twilight, though once in bright day, the glare of sun rushing to claim the world—what keeps returning to their thoughts, the images lingering and making their primitive claim. The water, if you close your eyes, is a messenger. But if you open your eyes, you see—beyond the creek and trees and the vacant lot—the brick ranch house of a neighbor with an asphalt driveway and a basketball hoop fastened above the garage. You can almost hear the thump thump thump of the basketball, almost see the high-school girl shooting baskets with her boyfriend. At the far edge of the yard is an enclosure of fence, two horses grazing. The horses appear ancient to the boys, enormous, bending down into the grass. And the girl, in their memories, sometimes goes up on her tiptoes to press her lips to the boy's lips—to make a seal the way dusk seals the horizon— or she walks hand in hand with the boy into the field and to the woods, glancing nervously behind her. And it is beside the mud water that it is possible to see them making of their clothes a lopsided pile amid the weeds. And what you see after that is a secret. You breathe it down into your lungs and hold it there, and the mosquitoes anoint you with blood, and the voices of the crickets fill the air with commotion.

The brothers are ten and nine that October, and they have lived in this same Ohio town for all their lives, in the same stucco house for as long as they can remember, as though the house and their lives are the same thing. Always they have a view out the back windows of the small escape of the narrow woods. The trees begin at the edge of the yard, extend only as far as a count of twenty or thirty steps, then across the fence is the open field with its broken bottles and candy wrappers. It is here where the boys feel most themselves, where they go to be free of the constraints of their mother and father. The boys, in the clearing, possess the wildness of their voices, the rocks or dirt balls that they hold in their hands, and a fierce current of emotions. Once they struck a squirrel with a rock so the creature dropped from a limb, then quickly ran off. Another time they heard the desperate mewling of what turned out to be a matted fluff of a kitten. With a stick they held the animal beneath the surface of the creek, a baptism, watching the rushing waters moving off into their slow eternity.

The boys, now, don't know how to stop walking this way to get to school, how not to return to this place when the day is done, slipping from their house while the last of day is draining from the sky, hiding in the trees and watching the creek and the driveway and the basketball hoop. It is disappointing, though, how everything is as quiet and uneventful as the space between heartbeats. Sometimes, after rain, the boys see raccoon prints in the mud, scrawled like a strange and mystical writing, or they see the creek swell to a furious height, picking up speed. And they know to look at the ground as they cross the tiny bridge that arches its back over the creek, and they hold their thoughts in abeyance while remembering the paleness of the bodies writhing, making noises that might be pain or wonder. But there is nothing here now in October, so they keep walking through the rush of dead leaves.

They are wearing windbreakers. Probably the temperature will warm as the day goes on, but for now the breezes are an anger, rising and falling. Jason is the older of the boys, though everyone calls him Jay, which he likes because his mother says that a blue jay is the most devious of birds, along with crows, which sometimes oar out above the canopy in the woods. The crows are large enough that they want to blot out the sky, but not so large that they can. Seth, the younger brother, is no longer thinking of the woods behind him, not now that they have crossed through it. He would have to turn around to remember it, but already they are late to school, and in any case there is the wind to think about, how it presses against you, like a strict hand. Jay, on the other hand, imagines that he carries the place inside him as he walks, and he will horde it all the way to school and into Homeroom. It is like the scaffolding of bones inside the body. He is still thinking about this when they arrive at the school baseball field, near where they once saw a dead baby mouse.

"Don't walk inside with me," Jay says to his younger brother. They are moving toward the cracked sidewalk that will lead them to the main entrance. But Seth is already slipping ahead, picking up speed, and Jay is pausing. He can't quite move his body forward, not while he is looking behind him, peering in the direction of the distant trees.

THE BOYS KNOW THERE are rules, and they are absolute. It is Sunday, early in the evening. The world appears dull gray through the windows of their bedroom, as though the sky is barely breathing, hibernating. They are sitting on the floor, cross-legged, playing Texas Hold 'em. The boys exist in the seam of the world, in the narrow slip where there has to be silence, where nothing else is possible. They shuffle the cards by spreading them on the carpeting and swirling them. They use pennies for chips but do not clink them. They whisper if they have to say a word. They know Father is downstairs in the living room, is lying on the couch without any lights. They know he has draped across his left eye a washcloth with ice cubes at their center. A migraine is gnawing inside Father's head like a living creature, behind his left eye. And they understand what will happen if they dare venture downstairs, if they walk into the kitchen where their mother is probably smoking at the kitchen table, if they open a cupboard or turn on a light or speak in even a normal-sounding voice.

Jay is losing to his younger brother, which shouldn't happen. He can't keep his mind focused on the way the cards are moving in and out of sight before him, flashing their faces. He is thinking, instead, about the smoke from his mother's cigarette lifting its gray-blue body to curl across the kitchen ceiling. And he is thinking about the place in the woods and the now-distant summer, what it felt like to stand witness in the growing dark of the woods.

"Your deal," Seth says.

"What?" Jay asks.

"Your turn."

Jay feels the cards beneath his fingers as he swirls them. He thinks of Braille you can supposedly read by touching it, but these cards are so slick to the touch you might hold them in your hands forever and never learn a thing.

Jay says, "Let's sneak out."

"What?"

"We can go out the back door."

"Now?"

"We need coats," he says.

One of Jay's earliest memories is of the cemetery where they buried Grandma Muriel. All the dead were lying there inside the earth, holding their breaths. Now he and Seth hold their breaths until they are clear of the house, clear of the yard. It seems that the sky is wrapped in a dark gray sheet. There are birds flickering overhead, or maybe bats. The boys smell the mud of the earth, as old, it seems, as the bodies in the ground. Their feet scatter dead leaves. They walk into the dullness of the woods, the birds or bats with their silent soliloquies above them. They walk and walk until they reach the wet breath of creek, then Seth breaks the silence to say, "They won't be out here."

"I know," Jay says.

"They aren't coming back."

"Follow me," Jay says.

"Where?"

They have never before ventured to the permanence of the house itself, to the brick edifice, have never crossed by the rail fence near the great bodies of the horses, the smell of them like something hiding in a dense and moist cave. There is grass beneath their feet, the smudge of the basketball hoop affixed to the garage, the ghost of a net that sways and appears alive in the wind. The brick walls of the house are hard and cold against their palms. A house is a map to follow, so they swirl around it, moving past the dull glow behind the curtains, and a sliding glass door. They notice a blue flickering sea of a television, distorted and wraithlike. Jay is reminded of when you close your eyes in summer and see the bright pink of sunlight against your eyelids.

Everywhere around the house there are more curtains or blinds or darkness. But there is one room near the back of the low-slung home where a spectral voice exists inside the bricks, mumbling there, squawking. Only after a moment do they realize it is music, turned low. They touch their ears close to the window glass—the veil of dark curtains cleaves—but the music is no more decipherable than the images of the television, no more corporeal.

"It's freezing," Seth says. "Let's go home."

"Keep your voice down."

Then—and later it will seem the smallness of a miracle, a fissure into some other world—a light to their left opens its insect eye. At once the boys move toward it, leaning close, their faces pressed so near they see through the tiny slats in the blinds. There is a rounded white sink and mirror, a shower curtain with stains or blotches that might be flowers, and then the girl herself. They have never been so near to her, never seen her through such a tiny aperture of horizon. She has long blond hair parted straight down the middle, where, along the narrow creek of it, there is a darker mud color. She is wearing jeans and a sweatshirt and has bare feet. This is the body they saw offering itself in the summer to the boy, his movements like a moth battering against an outdoor light. Now the girl's hands undo the button to her jeans, the zipper. She is sitting, then, with the exposed nakedness of her upper legs, on the toilet, casually tearing a bit of toilet paper from the roll, holding it like rosary beads. The boys, of course, are in a thrall. Then the girl is reaching down between her legs, wiping. Then she begins to stand, lifting the underwear straddled on her upper legs to cover her, lifting her jeans, and flushing the toilet—all in one smooth, practiced motion, a magician's spell.

The boys are running after that. Running into the triumph of the moonlight that appears now on the grass like a fine mist. And they are laughing, a sound as old to their ears as the cawing of birds.

FATHER, TODAY, IS SITTING at the kitchen table, drinking. The boys' mother is there with him, though it's mainly Father's voice that lifts to the ceiling and lurks there with the mother's cigarette smoke. Father broods like the discarded skin of a snake when he is drunk, and Jay remembers a black snake they found once curled beneath the porch, the feral flickering of a tongue. Jay, now, is sitting at the bottom of the stairs leading up to the second floor, listening to the voices of Father and Mother float out of the kitchen and make their way into the house. Twice now Seth has come to the top of the stairs and asked Jay to play, but Jay wants to stay where he is, wants to lean his cheek against the railing while the voices pass through his body.

"Come up and watch TV," Seth says again.

"Later," Jay says.

"What are you doing down there?"

"Dad is mad," Jay says.

"About what?"

"I don't know."

Later, after dark, the boys sneak out. The ritual is that Jay says yes and Seth says it's too cold, but finally gives in. Now there is the first snow of the season falling from the sky. It seems, almost, that the moon must have broken into pieces and is sifting down, forming a language, its words covering the earth.

And then the boys are walking through it, dressed in coats and gloves and shoes. They have done this a half dozen times since spotting the girl squatting down, but most nights there is nothing, nothing. Just the curtains at the house, the blinds. Just a few muted sounds beyond the walls.

"This is stupid," Seth says on this night.

OUT THE WINDOWS OF Father's car today there is so much speeding by, but inside the Toyota everyone is holding still. Jay is thinking about the neighborhood houses with their driveways and trash cans perching by the road, is thinking about his mother in her church clothes, smoking. Tension fills the car the way water fills a bathtub once you plug it, rising and rising. Jay is watching Father's free right arm, which is draped across the seat, poised. The trick is to watch Father's hand for the first twitch. Seth is still yammering, unhappy he is missing his cartoons. And any second it will happen. And then it does. The hand lashes out, aiming for Seth's face but missing, striking Jay instead, even though Jay sees it coming, even though he tries to duck away. There is blood he tastes in his mouth, pooling there the way the sounds of the bells pool in the neighborhood around the church.

That night, when they are supposedly in bed, asleep, Jay and his brother walk into the woods. The leaves crunch their complaint beneath their shoes, speaking in muttering voices. At one point Jay leans against a dead shagbark hickory, closes his eyes, and imagines you might hear a voice rising from the night and burrowing into your body. Then he and Seth cross to the house and make their pattern of rounding it. Only on the second circuit do they see the light blurring in the bathroom, see through the narrow slat the closed shower curtain, hear the battering of water. They wait and wait, are vessels. Then a naked arm of the girl reaches for a blue towel, and soon the curtain flies open, and they see, in that instant, the dark center eyes of her breasts, the nest between her legs. Jay cannot bring himself to breathe, and suddenly there is a sound beside him, and he realizes his brother has reached up and is pounding his knuckles to the glass. They are running, then, running through a dream of snow, running with the furious clouds of their breaths.

"Why did you do that?" Jay asks once they reach the woods.

"It was funny," Seth says.

"We could have watched her."

"Did you see her jump?" he asks.

"You idiot," Jay says. "Now we can't go back. You made sure of that."

"So?" Seth asks.

"So you're an idiot."

"Shut up," Seth says.

"No, you do," Jay says, and they are walking again back to their own house, moving forward the way you know to even if your eyes are closed, one foot gliding before the other.

FATHER IS CHOPPING WOOD in the backyard. The boys hear the persistence of the axe, which tears into the fabric of the hour. It is Saturday. The boys feel boredom wrapping around them, insinuating itself into their bodies, which are lethargic on the couch as they watch television. Jay's thoughts, as always, drift at one point to images of the girl beside the passage of the creek, the boy pressing his weight against her. He sees, too, her hands on her bare legs as she sits on the toilet, her damp body as the shower curtain falls away. He feels these images slipping beneath his skin, lingering. He and Seth have stayed away for days and days and days. They have been exiled, banished, as though the space of their lives has been too small, narrowed down to nothing. Only in the last week have they begun sneaking back, and Jay feels the lure of it, the pull. Seth always shrugs or complains, but still they go. There is nothing of any interest most nights—just the black resistance of the house walls in the darkness—but it doesn't matter.

On this night, after dark, in bitter cold, after their parents have left to go to Red Lobster, after the house belongs to them and to no one else, they begin to argue.

"It's too far," Seth says. "It's stupid."

"There's nothing else to do," Jay says.

"It's cold."

"Maybe we'll see something."

"So what?"

"We have to go," Jay says. "We're going."

And the wind, it turns out, seems to want to wash away the old world to make a new one. And the woods are huddled low, a drift of stars existing so far above them they seem like an afterlife, fixed in the dark waters.

They arrive at the house, then make a first round. A thin paste of snow persists on the grass. The house is a closed history, Jay imagines, a locked mouth, sealed, existing unchanging while days and weeks and years slip past. And it is only on the second circle that they realize that the only car at the house—they go up on tiptoes to peer into the dusty world of the garage—is parked by the street. A blue Ford. Ancient. And though there is a light in the bathroom where they spotted the girl in the past, now there is only the pale sink to keep itself company, the empty shower, the mute seat of the toilet. It is only, in fact, at the sliding glass door that they notice any signs of life at all. They hear the murmuring of the television, speaking in tongues, see the blue flickering sea on closed curtains. If they stand close enough, they spy where the wrinkled seam of curtains softens, opens. And inside the living room there are only a few moving notes of light, images that bloom and recede. And there on the couch—Jay sees it first so nudges Seth—the boyfriend is lying atop the girl. The brothers watch, transfixed. Jay remembers once seeing a catfish dragged into a rowboat by his father, thrashing as though trying to free itself from its own body. The boy and girl move like that. Then, almost at once, they stop, and the boy stands from the couch, a swollenness between his legs. He is dressing, then, and the girl is dressing, and Jay watches them bathed in flickering light, illuminated like a watching eye. It is then that Jay slips in his balance and bangs his forehead with a firm thump against the glass. The half-naked boy comes toward them at once, the glass door receding. He is stepping out. Then the boys are running, running.

Later—at home, in bed—Jay will recall what he saw next, as though from a high perch. He and Seth are in full sprint away from the house, the boy with only his pants to cover him, calling out something in the cold. And Seth, not seeing the retaining wall at the far edge of the house, bangs his knee and tumbles down, sprawling. And the enormous boy grabs hold and fixes Seth in place. The boy is shouting words, expulsions of sound. And Seth is squirming, so Jay crashes his body into the wall of the boy, knocking him sideways. Then Jay and his brother are running again toward the woods, the fallen boy upright and in pursuit, the footsteps behind them clambering. But soon there are only their own footsteps, only the dense sprawl of the trees, the valve of night opening and closing. And not until they are back in the white glare of their mother's kitchen does Jay see that blood drops are slipping onto Mother's floor.

"She'll kill us if she sees that," Jay says.

"I was cut by the wall," Seth says.

"Go back outside."

"No."

"Do you know how much trouble we'll be in?"

"We're never going back to that house," Seth says. "Not ever. You have to promise that."

Jay hesitates, then says, "Okay."

He is down on his hands and knees now with paper towels, scrubbing. Here are the blood smears, the reproach of the words he has spoken bitter into the air. And it's true, he knows. They can't go back. Ever. It is over, like the prayers their Mother makes them mouth Sundays in church, prayers rising toward the rafters, insisting. But surely those prayers must die beyond the treetops, slip back to earth, catch in the fields or in the rivers. Jay cannot say what is coming with his future, except for the space of the days ahead, their geography. He will be as old someday as the boy and girl, will know whatever mysteries they know, will understand or not understand, like in the night when he wakes sometimes to hear the forlorn slapping of the tree branches rubbing up against the eaves outside the bedroom, squeaking. Over the summer, he remembers, he once saw a hawk rising on the road near their house, lifting from the entrails of a raccoon, a pickup whooshing near. The bird started too late, twisting in the air when the front of the pickup struck it, sending it twirling and thrashing down into the bar ditch. Jay ran to see the creature lying there. It was in the tall grass, unlocked of its body, offering a few final twitches before lying still. Jay imagines the years like that, swarming and flying, then being motionless, and he rises from the floor and throws the wad of bloodied paper towels into the trash.

The Second Coming

Eugene's earliest memory is of his father beating a man nearly to death on the street outside their apartment building in West Chicago. The beating itself is a little fuzzy, but Gene does remember clearly—or believes he remembers—the blood on his father's hands and shirt, the injured man on his back and moaning on the sidewalk. Apparently the man had permanent brain damage from the beating, and Gene's father went to prison. It was just as well, their mother always said. The family was better off. There were three children total, and their mother worked as a waitress and sometimes cleaned motel rooms and once worked for a week at a camera shop as a cashier. She made a point of often reminding her children that their father was no good, that he could pretend to be charming, but it was all an act. She told them that if he ever got out of prison they should have nothing to do with him, under no circumstances. It was the one certain truth of the family, the only thing all of them accepted without bickering or strife, and it followed them to different neighborhoods in the city, through the hard times of never having enough money. In Gene's mind his father was a great brute of a man, not even fully human, a strange beast. In truth he couldn't recall what his father looked like beyond the blood on his hands and shirt, beyond the way he'd stood over that hopeless man on the sidewalk, kicking him. It was a terrible memory, and he assumed that his father was the stuff of nightmares. He also knew, though, that life with his mother was difficult in its own right, especially after she came down with diabetes. She was tired all the time now but needed to work longer hours because of the medical bills. In April that year she didn't have enough money for rent, and it seemed likely they would be evicted soon if that didn't change. Gene didn't want to live on the street. His mother took the family to the church on Newton that Sunday so they could pray, and what Gene prayed for was that Jesus would pay the rent for them, at least for a little while, and that the diabetes would disappear. Jesus cured the blind and the lepers and the people who couldn't walk, after all. Diabetes seemed a simple matter next to things like that. Surely it was easier than walking on water or bringing the dead back to life. And it wasn't even four days after those prayers—Gene was leaving the school yard—when a man approached him. The man was skinny and looked old, with long Jesus hair. His teeth were bad, and his breath smelled. He told Gene he was his father, which at first was hard to understand. Because the man looked like Jesus, Gene wondered if he meant that he was a priest or maybe God the Father, and that's what he wanted to be called. But the man started saying that he was out of prison now and knew he wasn't supposed to see his kids, but he just couldn't help himself. He told Gene he wanted forgiveness. He told him he loved him. Gene, of course, was scared now—he looked at his father's hands for blood, his father's shirt for blood—but then the man handed him some money from his pocket, a handful of wadded-up and dirty bills. Only later did Gene count the bills and realize it was nearly two hundred dollars, enough to keep the landlord at bay for another month or at least part of one. It was a miracle, he knew, but at once he had a dilemma. He went home and waited for his mother to return from work. He was sitting at the kitchen table when she came home, and, as usual, she seemed to know that something was wrong. When she gave him a look, he couldn't decide whether he was better off telling her that the money had come from his father or from Jesus. He kept going back and forth in this thinking, but then his mother grew impatient and started quizzing him, so he quickly showed her the money and told her it was Jesus who gave it to him. That seemed safer, in the end. It turned out his mother beat him for lying, but in any case Gene thought it was the wise choice, and she did take the money to give to the landlord. And as the years passed Gene decided it probably really had been Jesus after all, had been a miracle, even though his mother had her leg amputated not long after that because of her illness, even though his younger sister died from being hit by a bus in the street, even though they did live for a time in a shelter and almost never had enough money to keep their bellies full.

Spring Snow

I am not a superstitious man. I can say that with some confidence. It was my father who believed he could read into the world its future, who told me often in childhood that three crows in a willow tree were the worst omen, portending the death of a loved one, a serious illness of a neighbor, or a miscarriage for a cousin. He seemed to think there was a hidden numerology in nature, and often I saw him counting blue-jay feathers left without warning on the grass, or tallying blood drops dotting the snow come winter, or lining up pairs of dead frogs floating in the shallows of the river beyond the barn.

I do not doubt the fervor of those beliefs, but I do wish sometimes I might resurrect my father from the grave long enough to explain the inconsistencies and illogic of his interpretations, which often shifted depending on the state of his sobriety or general mood, as contradictory as spring snow. I count as my earliest memory the man carrying a dead buck on his shoulders while a few errant flakes were falling. He lugged the creature past new flowers rising from the earth, ferrying the animal out from the woods by our rural Ohio home. This was not unlike the way he sometimes lifted me high above the world, saddled on his shoulders, hauling me past my mother, then up the stairs to my bedroom. I see him dropping the deer onto the grass, kneeling before it, then drawing his knife from sternum to crotch, blood welling from what seemed a secret opening, the intestines slipping free. I do not know if my father thought it was possible to read in those entrails what was coming, though surely, had he managed it, he would have seen in his own few remaining years only drunkenness, a meanness of spirit, and a general pervasive failure. What I mostly recall about that distant morning is gazing into the deer's glassy eyes, the creature oblivious to the violation taking place down below, as though death were a kind of hypnotic state that helps you rise above even the most profound of indignities.

There was a time when I would have insisted that the only appropriate response to some parents is hatred, but few things are actually that simple. Is it actually possible to tease such feelings free from love or indifference or anger or disappointment or bemusement? Perhaps, if I am honest, my responses to my father have existed always on their own strange yet predictable orbit, moving forever through their stages, not unlike the man himself disappearing from our lives for weeks or even months on end, though always returning, parking his pickup in the garage, then stepping through the back door without apology or explanation, peering into the refrigerator to snare a Pabst Blue Ribbon, as though it were normal for a husband and father to live as often gone from the house as with his family.

The first time I remember him vanishing for more than a few days, I was nine or maybe ten. This was not long after a white oak was felled by lightning fifty feet from the house, the explosion awakening us in the darkness, catapulting us from bed. The next morning my father and I walked together to the fallen trunk, which hadn't yet realized it had died, the greenery sprawling across the earth not far from the cistern. Often, in those days, I heard the voices of my parents in the walls, their anger vibrating or maybe rocking me into sleep—is it possible to grow so accustomed to rancor that it seems a form of comfort?— so I can't say for certain whether it was the sight of that severed oak or some dispute with my mother that caused him to carry his suitcase out to his pickup, then drive away, the tires kicking up gravel. But I do remember him standing that morning by the majestic fallen tree and saying, "Let's not pretend this is anything good, Frankie. We should brace ourselves. All you can do in life is make yourself ready for whatever is coming."

"Maybe it's a good sign," I said.

"No," he said. "It's not."

It is easier, we know, to forgive someone in their absence, and so in the six weeks my father was gone on this occasion, I thought of him almost every day, worrying over his separation from our lives in the way a tongue might forage for that empty slot where a tooth has been yanked away. Often, in the old days, he would take me hunting, mostly for squirrels, and I missed that moment when I would hold my breath and gaze down the barrel, when I would squeeze the trigger, and the squirrel would drop like a dead weight to the earth, making an audible thump my father would reward by slapping me enthusiastically on the back. Other times he let me sit in his lap and work the steering wheel of his pickup, pressing his boot against the accelerator until the fields rushing past seemed to blur beyond recognition, becoming part of no world I knew . . . other than the mystical one he always seemed to be imagining when the wind kicked up dust devils by the bar ditches in August, or a wild violet grew through the eye socket of a half-buried possum skull in our backyard.

"Is he ever coming back?" I asked my mother one evening, but her answer to most questions was to squint into the cigarette smoke rising into her eyes, the ash lengthening until finally it crumbled beneath its own weight.

I remember spying one early dawn in July, a coyote running through the backyard by my mother's tomato plants. The coyote had three legs, which reminded me of how my father had limped since falling from the barn roof two summers earlier, his upper thigh suffering such a serious hematoma it seemed that it would never heal. It is an art and not a science to read what is coming in the signs around us—or so my father claimed—but still I grew convinced that at any moment I would see his pickup sputtering up the driveway toward the garage, would hear the back screen door slamming, his boots being kicked off, and the television being turned up too loud.

But it wasn't until much later that summer that he returned, and I recall running out the front door and leaping from my feet into his arms. He swung me around, though surely I was too old for such displays. That same day I was asked to wash his truck with the hose, to wax it until it shimmered in the sunlight, and he made the request in a way that left little possibility for refusal.

"And if you're going to do it," he said, "why not at least put in the effort and make it truly shine?"

Over the years of my childhood, I remember my father working drywall jobs and roofing jobs and carpenter jobs, but mostly I recall him talking about the bad state of the economy and how difficult it was to find any work that paid a living wage, then arguing with my mother over how she ought to raise the rates she charged the neighboring farmers to exploit her land. The farm itself had been passed down to my mother from her grandparents, and it supplied her with barely enough cash to pay off the property taxes and to keep her in hamburger and Pall Malls. Still, she seemed to find little motivation to stray from the land except for the occasional trip to the grocery and liquor stores. Each day at dusk she treated herself to a cocktail composed of gin, lime juice, and seltzer. My father wasn't back home for that cocktail hour for even a full week before the arguments began, mostly because he spotted one evening at dusk a small brown bat trying to burrow beneath the bark of a shagbark hickory. He insisted he was being told by the universe that my mother ought to get out more, that she ought to join him for an evening of drinking or even dancing in town, and maybe even head out on a family vacation to Mackinac Island in Michigan.

"We can't afford it," she said.

"Then sell the damn farm. What good is it doing you?"

"I'm not selling it."

"Sell it and invest the money," he said. "That's the only way to get ahead. It's what the thieving bankers do. Why not join them?"

"So the trip to Mackinac is an investment?"

"For God's sake, Jenny, stop being a total cheapskate. You could out-Jew a Jew."

"I'm not selling."

"Why don't you just sit at this table, then, and smoke your cigarettes for the next forty years? That sounds like quite the life. Think how envious everyone will be. You can die knowing you experienced everything the world had to offer."

The argument—as always with my parents—flared and died over many days. Once, I remember, they argued for weeks over whether it was acceptable for a husband to take a few dollars from his wife's purse without asking, if that was or wasn't part of the marital compact. My mother's view was my father was a leech, the kind that on occasion affixed themselves to my ankles when I went wading into the sluggish parts of the river at the edges of the farm, leeches I burned off with the glowing red tip of a match. My father was home for not even a month when the worst argument that season sprang up between them. I was eating Rice Krispies in the kitchen when I heard my father's voice lumbering out in anger from upstairs, my mother's voice answering in kind. Usually I ignored such displays, paying no more attention than to the sounds of the Norfolk Southerns in the distance, but the tone this time demanded that I climb the narrow stairs of the old farmhouse, linger in the open doorway to my parents' room.

My father was pointing at a fissure in the window glass beside the bed, a jagged slice about the length of a finger.

"How long has this been here?" he asked.

"How the hell would I know?" my mother said.

"You were unfaithful . . . weren't you?"

"What are you talking about?"

"While I was gone. You had some other man up in this bed. Don't lie to me. I know it happened."

"You're insane, Joe. You are absolutely out of your mind."

"I know what I know," he said, adding, "So how many times did you fuck someone in this bed?"

My mother shot a glance in my direction before turning back to her husband, saying, "You see, Joe—don't you—that Francis is standing right there in that doorway?"

"Well," my father said, "it's only right he knows that his mother is a whore."

"Why? Because some bird probably banged against the window and cracked it a little? Or maybe the glass is just old. Are you sure you're not retarded, Joe? There's been more and more evidence over the years in that direction."

"Tell me the truth, Frank," my father said. "Was she bringing a man in here like a cheap slut?"

"She never has anybody over," I said.

"Don't try to reason with him, Francis. It's like trying to reason with a pig turd. It doesn't have the capacity."

"You couldn't wait a few weeks while I was gone," my father said. "What kind of example is that to show for your son?"

"Oh, you're right, Joe. I confess. I had a different man in here every day and night, sometimes several at a time. They were sticking things where I didn't even know they would fit. I'm not sure what half of them were doing."

"You have a filthy mouth," he said.

"You don't think it's bad enough to let you on top of me?" she said. "I think I've had my fill for a lifetime. It's overrated, if you ask me."

"You're lying," my father said. "You're lying to my face, and I won't stand for it. I have half a mind to slap you around a little."

"Well," she said, "you certainly have built yourself a strong case. There's no denying that. There's a little crack in the glass of the window. I must be a Jezebel. Case closed."

"You did it," he said. "I know you did."

"Fuck you, Joe."

"I always knew you couldn't be trusted."

"Are you kidding me?" she said. "You're the one who runs off to your brothers or God knows where. Who knows what you've been up to? I'm surprised it hasn't fallen off yet from some disease or another."

"Don't push me," he said. "You're right up at the edge."

Three days later my father was gone again, the spot for his truck in the garage empty except for a few oil drops. I sneaked sometimes into my mother's bedroom to marvel over the small break in the glass, how something so seemingly inconsequential could tell you everything there was to know about a life. This time, though, I told myself not to fall into the same mistake, not to keep wishing for my father to return and to take me again into the woods with the rifle. I told myself we were better off without him, should be relieved to have the quiet of the evenings and nights. I reminded myself that hatred has its proper place in the world. This time, it turned out, I didn't see my father for more than a year, but I kept telling myself it was better like this, better for everyone, including my mother, who began seeing a man named Dennis Morgan, who worked at the plastics plant in the next county but who drove two hours every weekend to be with her, to climb the stairs to her bed beside that little fissure in the glass. It occurred to me, of course, that reading the signs involved a little guesswork—my father would be the first to admit that—and perhaps he had simply gotten the timeline confused. The new man, Dennis, had the good sense never to treat me like a son or to presume any familial connection. He came to be with my mother, to make her moan in the bed while I was attempting to sleep past the thin wall, to smoke and drink with her on the back porch, then to head back to work and to his home. The next time my father came back, in the dead of winter, my mother said she would call the police if he tried to stay, and after that I didn't see him for another two years, though I did hear the crows calling often from the fields behind the house, and I counted them sometimes when they gathered in the trees or spread out like strange dark obelisks in the distance.

The final time I saw him he was in an open casket in Mercer County, not far from the Indiana border. I drove there with my mother to pay our respects. My father's brothers resented that we were there, but my mother started talking on the drive back following the funeral—we were on the road for nearly three hours—telling me how much she had once loved the man when they'd first met, how sweet and boyish he had seemed, how his love of the natural world had made him seem connected to something primitive, so true, as basic as the mud of the earth. It was snowing beyond the windshield of the car, light flakes that didn't have the energy to cling when they landed, so simply disappeared, as though they had never existed in the first place. She lit cigarettes as she drove, the butts congregating in the open ashtray, the red of her lipstick staining the tips like a faint blood. Not often this talkative, my mother spoke fondly of the man while smoke from her cigarettes rose in the car like a strange cloud or veil, her words lifting and swirling around us like a small and peaceful storm. And the longer she spoke, the more I realized we were safe at long last, that we didn't have to worry any more, that the days of listening for the pickup in the driveway or the banging of the screen door were finally gone, that I could love my father now if I wanted, could speak of him with whatever appreciation and sympathy and affection I might want.

Little Dancer Aged Fourteen

I t was the third and final day of the NFDA convention in Chicago, and weary of the panels and PowerPoint slides, I slipped away for the afternoon to visit the Art Institute, where I stood in open awe before works by Manet, Monet, and Morisot . . . though in all honestly it was the sculpture *Little Dancer Aged Fourteen*, by Degas, that left me somehow weakened with wonder, as though beauty were a kind of aesthetic flu. I know that sounds like an exaggeration, but my youngest child—Lucy—had left back in August for college in Austin, Texas, far from home, and I think the girl Degas created nearly two centuries earlier reminded me of her when she was younger. I was still wobbling a little beneath the weight of that emotion when I headed down the stairs at the front of the building and found myself faced with a sudden impediment to my path—a boy who couldn't have been more than fourteen himself. And here's the thing: he pressed a dark handgun into my belly and asked for my wallet, my cell phone, my watch. Earlier that morning I had attended a session on how to deal with belligerent and irrational grievers who took out their sorrow and pain on those of us who were only there to help, and the session had sparked, at the end, some of the most impassioned dialogue I had ever heard from any collection of people in my profession—we are mostly a reserved lot—but now this boy seemed furious to the point of stuttering, and he wore a green stocking cap and had brown, dirty, stringy hair slipping out from underneath it, and his skin was so pale I knew I would touch it up if I were preparing him for burial. I can't explain it, but suddenly I imagined this poor boy on the table before me back in Highland Park, and we had reached the stage in the embalming process where I was suturing his mouth closed— threading the needle into the jaw, then up into one nostril and septum, then down into the other nostril and back into the mouth . . . an act I had performed so many hundreds of times I could do it in my sleep—and I felt such sadness for this child it was almost more than I could bear, particularly when combined with the emotions I had experienced inside the museum when I had gazed at the sculpture of the girl with her arms behind her back, one foot forward and tilted to the side, chin up, and I had realized that the model who had posed for the work was now a dusty pile of bones in a distant grave, if that, and yet once she had danced with enough enthusiasm and precision to inspire Degas to cast her into art that would persist for ages after she was gone. And yet this poor boy with his gun would not likely be preserved in anyone's memory—at least not for very long—and perhaps that was why he seemed so enraged to stand before me, screaming. And here's the part that isn't easy to explain: I had been transported by beauty and sadness so far from any visceral experience of the moment that I seemed to be watching from above, and what I saw was my own inert body standing on the steps, my arms slackened at my sides, as though I were the one who had died and not the girl who was Degas's model, my navy-blue tie a little askew at my neck, my gray eyes behind my glasses blinking and blinking. But what I wasn't doing was handing the child the items he was seeking, nor was I answering him when he shouted in my direction and jabbed at my stomach. And the part that no one believes when I tell this story, that I'm not sure I believe myself, particularly since I recall it like a strange dream, is that I reached down and gently stroked the boy's cheek, as though to comfort him. He ducked away at once as though my hand were a kind of flame, and he'd been seared, and then he was running down the steps and sidewalk, and I found myself for a moment going after him, not running but walking quickly, and I have no idea why on earth I did that or what I would have said should he have turned around again to face me.

Water Tower

T. J.'s earliest memories were of how the tower lifted toward the sky outside his bedroom, and how, at the back of his grandmother's house, in his tiny room with a mattress on the floor and one narrow window, he could see past the clothesline and wooden fence to the great structure. Sometimes it was a mechanical giant with multiple legs reaching down to earth, and other times it was a spaceship of aliens from a distant planet nothing like our own, a planet, perhaps, where everyone lived high on stilts above the grass, higher, even, than the trees. The fat body of the ship was rusted with age, as though the alien beings had been inside and watching for a very long time. Perhaps they lived for thousands of years and moved so slowly that, to them, it seemed they had just landed. Maybe, inside, they were preparing themselves to come out and to conquer all humanity, but there wasn't any hurry, so life went on.

T. J., when he was little older, would drink and smoke sometimes beneath the water tower, and it was there he spoke with Deanna for the first time. She came walking past with her dog, Podunk, on a leash. It was a mutt dog, not much larger than a rat, and had a high, frenetic bark or maybe yelp. T. J. knew Deanna from school—she was Clifton's little sister—and he and his friends threw empty beer bottles in her direction and yelled that she should strip for them or they'd rip off her clothes and make her go home naked.

"Not that you have anything to show off," he called out.

"Fuck you," Deanna said.

One of the mysteries of the water tower was the graffiti. When T. J. was younger he would wonder how it got there. Weeks or even months would pass with no change, but then suddenly some new obscenity or gang symbol would find its way one morning high above the neighborhood. When he was very young he thought it was the aliens speaking in their own obscure language, but when he was older he marveled instead about how high someone had to climb to get there. He thought about climbing someday himself, but the truth was he suspected it might spoil things. The water tower was a mystery, a beautiful mystery—even though his grandmother referred to it as an "eyesore TV antenna"—and he thought it was best to keep a certain reverent distance.

The first time T. J. sold Deanna heroin he was seventeen. She was fifteen and knocked on his bedroom window. She had dark hair and big eyes—they had a way of capturing him in their grip, holding his attention the way the moon did when it perched some nights behind the water tower—and he lifted the screen so she could poke her head and shoulders inside.

He said, "If you don't have the money you can pay in trade."

"I have money."

"You don't want to come in?"

"No."

His father was out of prison then, visiting, and it was that same weekend they both heard the sirens. They were sitting at the kitchen table, drinking.

"What the fuck is that about?" his father asked.

It turned out some teenager from three blocks over had climbed to the top of the water tower and had jumped to his death. T. J. could think about little else for many days—it even eclipsed his thoughts about Deanna. He didn't know the kid who jumped but could picture him climbing up and up, standing behind the railing for a moment and looking down. The railing circled the tower a little above where the tank itself first began. When he was younger, T. J. pretended that the aliens would probably be standing there the first time anyone saw them; but, instead, on this occasion, it was the suicide who stood there. At some point he must have climbed the railing and jumped— maybe a swan dive—and splatted to his death. Later that day, after the ambulance and police cars had left, T. J. and his father walked over to see if there was blood or bits of body parts, but there wasn't anything of any particular interest.

In one of his dreams, T. J. imagined fastening explosives to each of the legs of the tower and blowing it out of the sky. He imagined it crashing down to earth, the great tank splitting open so he could climb in and discover the mysteries inside.

He told that story to Deanna once. She had missed her vein with the first try with the needle—no blood came pouring in— and she was trying again. The black tar was low quality but better than nothing.

She said, "You're a fucking idiot."

"What are you talking about?"

"You blow that thing over you'll flood the whole neighborhood and drown."

"That doesn't make sense," he said.

"It's a *water* tower," she said. "What do you think is in it?"

As odd as it might seem to say, that fact had never occurred to him before. But it *was* a water tower . . . that's what everybody called it. If he had known that when he was younger, he suspected, he would have imagined that the aliens were a kind of fish or maybe an octopus that came to earth and meant to hit the oceans but missed . . . so were stuck for eternity in their own little tank.

Occasionally T. J. would wonder when he first realized he was in love with Deanna, and his most common theory was that it happened when he was thirteen, after he got out of the hospital from having been shot in the left thigh. There was some thought he might lose the leg—apparently they couldn't find a pulse for a time below the knee—and he was bedridden at home and at the mercy of his grandmother to come in to feed him and to help him down the hall to the bathroom. That gave him a lot of time to think. Often it was about the water tower, of course—if he lifted himself even slightly in bed he could see it out the window—but it was also about Deanna. There was a rumor going around that she'd given Marvin Seawall a blowjob beneath the viaduct on 7th, and that started him thinking about how pretty her lips were when she was cursing in the playground at school.

After the teenager committed suicide, an enclosed pen with a large padlock was placed around the bottom part of the ladder, but new graffiti kept appearing every few months anyway, which was a marvel. There was something strangely inspiring about the tower—how it stood so high above the rest of the neighborhood, godlike in its dominion over things, never going anywhere or doing anything, but still seeming majestic.

His grandmother died at age fifty-eight, from emphysema. T. J. was twenty-two. After she was buried he sold the house and moved in with a friend on Tomlin Avenue. The friend's apartment had a spare bedroom that looked out on the back of the bowling alley. After that he rarely saw the water tower—or Deanna for that matter—but sometimes he would go back to the old neighborhood for the nostalgia of it. He would look up at the tower and wonder how he had ever believed that aliens would put up with living in a place like that, and he would remember Deanna walking there with her dog so many years earlier.

The fact was he didn't actually sleep with her for the first time until he was nineteen. She was up on Bing Street in red short-shorts and leaning into car windows. He paid her with a combination of cash and a little bit of black tar, and they went back to his grandmother's house. Her body wasn't too beat up yet, and at the very end he looked out the window and saw the water tower, and he envisioned it—as he often had as a child— like a wondrous creation that was about to take flight and lift away forever from the earth.

Crow Death

Paul isn't certain how often he should think about his mother. She slips from his mind the way the sun slips into the woods behind the house. There are times when it is clear he is meant to think about her—when his father takes him to Rose Hill on the first Sunday of each new month—but there are other times when the rules are uncertain. More than a year has passed, and in that time his friends at school have come to say far less, if anything, and his teachers no longer pull him aside, kneel down to his height, and ask how he is doing. Everything is back the way it was, except now it is his father who stands with him at the bus stop every morning, who hands him his lunch box. His father also takes him hunting in the woods on weekends, more often than he used to in the past. It is winter now, and on this Friday after school they walk through the white snow into the woods. It is so cold their breath decides it is a cloud. Both he and his father shoot first at a squirrel on a limb at the far side of the creek, but miss. Then his father shoots at a fat black crow high in a white oak. It is a perfect shot—the bird comes tumbling down. There is blood on the snow. The black feathers and the white and the red are so vivid that Paul carries the memory with him back to the house. He thinks about it after his father puts him to bed that night, thinks about how still the crow looked there in the snow. Its eyes were glassy, like they weren't real. Paul has trouble sleeping from the memory, but at last he dreams that crows are calling from the distant trees. For a moment in the dream, he thinks this is his mother's voice.

Sometimes he can't picture her very clearly, but in his dreams he always knows that it is her. Often she sits beside him or kisses him on the forehead. There is a scent he recognizes—musky-sweet, like wildflowers deep in the woods. In the dream she lands on the grass beside him with a great shroud of dark wings. Something in that startles him, and suddenly he is awake once more. The tears come from nowhere, appearing of their own free choice. He rises from bed and crosses the hallway to find his father, but the bedroom door is flung open, the sheets on the bed thrown back, and no one is in there he can see. His father has a bathroom to himself, so Paul goes closer and hears the shower running. It seems his father is bathing in the middle of the night. Paul steps into the bathroom and pulls back the curtain to tell about his dream, but it's not his father there but his mother. The shower water is spraying down atop her. Her hair is dark black instead of reddish brown, much longer than he remembers. She turns, her eyes still closed as the water tumbles across her face. Then his father is behind him and yelling, and he is sent back to his room. Paul flings himself on the bed, only then realizing it wasn't his mother after all. He wills himself back into sleep, to burrow there. He wants to crawl inside his dream. He aches for his mother to fly down from the trees with her great wings.

Slippery Creek

When I was sixteen and living with my father for the final winter of his life, I fell in love for a time but did not mean to, and I lost something that was not mine to lose. Those were not happy times, that winter, but nor were they as sad as you might think, and in any case I am glad that they are over.

My father and I were living then on the sleepy banks of Slippery Creek, halfway between San Antonio and Austin. From our windows we could see the brown water rolling past, and we could hear it, too, and there were days when I grew weary of the sound and wished that we were living somewhere else. I know it sounds like I'm complaining, but the truth is there were worse places to be a boy and growing up. I had a room all to myself, a kerosene heater to keep me warm, and my father let me come and go as I pleased and enjoy a freedom that my high-school classmates only envied. Some might say that I was running wild down in Texas, and certainly there is some reason to believe that, but the truth is that I was not unlike many of my classmates at the high school, and there were worse things to be, in my opinion.

The high school I attended that winter was on the west end of Altoma Springs, and the bus ride home each day took us through the crowded neighborhoods close to town, past a large tool-and-dye plant, and then beyond the refinery with its blue flames and shiny metal holding tanks. But once we crossed Bethel Highway at the fairgrounds, the land opened up. There was something encouraging about the sight of those long, straight roads riding high above the drainage ditches, with nobody on them. By the time we bumped over the railroad tracks at Elora Ridge, most everyone had gotten off, and I walked slowly with my books in my arms, breathing in the winter air and feeling the sunlight trying to warm up the switchgrass and the mesquite. The outstretched arms of a live oak marked the spot of our cabin, which was slightly off the ground and had a wooden skirt with open slats painted white, with the river running off behind it. And as I walked there the thought sometimes came to me that anybody standing at that spot might think that the people living in that cabin were happy and that no harm would ever befall them. They were meant for good things and bright futures. I'm not sure that I agreed, but it was a promising feeling—no matter what was waiting down the road—and I carried it with me as I climbed up the stone stoop on a January afternoon, pulled out my house key, and unlocked the front door.

GARY WAPPELHORST WAS MY closest friend in Altoma Springs that winter, and the bus picked him up each morning shortly after me, picked him up at the Oneida Hills Trailer Park off Sprague Avenue. Gary would sit beside me on the bus, and there was a girl that winter named Rosaria Vasquez we would talk to sometimes. Rosaria was Mexican, of course—that was what we called them then—and she was fourteen and suffered from some strange astigmatism with her eyes so that when she looked at you it wasn't really at you, not precisely, which might sound unattractive but was the opposite. It was on the Monday after Christmas holidays when we first saw her—Rosaria, a freshman, was transferring over from St. Charles—very early in the morning, when the sky was mostly gray and the clouds were hugging low to the earth. One moment we were simply sitting there, and then the bus brakes moaned, the doors flew open with a whoosh, a gust of cold winter air went racing down the aisle, and there she was. Rosaria wasn't very tall—maybe 5'1" or 5'2"—and she had straight black hair and an almond complexion. I watched her look my way or maybe a little to my left, and then she settled into the seat just in front of us. I knew right then that something significant had happened, though I'm not sure I was happy that it had.

The next morning it was raining when I climbed from bed and dressed in the dark, when I fried my eggs over the wood stove, when I smoked a cigarette on the front porch, and when Gary and I first began talking to Rosaria on the school bus. Gary described how his family was originally from Fayetteville, Arkansas, and I explained how my father's many jobs had taken us since I was small to places like New Braunfels, San Antonio near Fort Sam Houston, Poteet, Little River, Killeen, Temple, Waco, and Round Rock. I remember that as we talked we passed through a neighborhood where the houses stood so close together they almost touched, and I remember seeing one house with a large American flag leaning out from the front porch, and I remember Rosaria telling me that her family had come originally from Montemorelos in Mexico and that her father believed in old-fashioned ways so sometimes slapped them. But I don't think I was listening very closely. What I remember most is the way the bus jiggled as we rode, and the way Rosaria jiggled as she spoke, and the way the rain kept coming down around us.

Then we rattled over the railroad tracks at Wendell Street, and everyone looked up and started stirring—we were close to the gravel entrance to the football field and school. After that we gathered up our things, sat up straight, and waited for the bus to stop. That is what our lives were like back then.

I SHOULD EXPLAIN THAT my father wasn't working. Franklin's Lumber Yard had let him go for supposedly stealing some paver bricks and other things. I am unsure how he spent his days while I was off at school, though I do know that he was rarely there when I came home. He was exactly six feet tall, rail thin, and had a pronounced Adam's apple, close-set eyes, and sandy hair that generally looked rumpled over breakfast. Sometimes late at night he would open a beer and phone my mother in Houston, though she was remarried then so generally hung up. For myself, I went out driving most nights into the countryside with Gary, and we would open the windows at seventy or even eighty miles an hour and feel the winter air rushing in. Other times we would drive out to Turtle Lake, sit in the back of the pickup, watch the yellow moon perching high above the water, and drink beer until we felt a little warmer. On a few nights, though, I would make an excuse to Gary, wait till it was dark, then make the long walk to the Del Mar Apartments. The apartments there were made of some kind of stucco, and there was a large trash bin I leaned against in the parking lot. I never knew for sure which bedroom Rosaria shared with her sisters, so I never knew if the shadows I saw on the shades belonged to her or someone else. That should have been discouraging, I suppose, but for some reason I always saw it as the opposite.

It was late one Sunday night after I returned home from those apartments that my father drove us into town for ice cream. "Are you coming?" he asked when I came through the front door. It was a clear, chilly night with bright stars, the recent rain behind us. The Ice Cream Shack was on Brower Road near the Liberty Baptist Church, and we pulled up and parked at the side by a stone wall. The other ice cream stores in town had closed for the winter, but not this one. We stamped our hands and feet to keep warm, ordered hot fudge sundaes, and ate them in the truck with the motor running. I could see through the side mirror the exhaust whipping up into the air, then disappearing, and it occurred to me that this might be just the kind of night I would remember when I was grown up and had a son or daughter of my own. And I was right, of course, though not for the reasons I was thinking.

On the ride home, just as we reached Old Highway 17, my father turned down the radio and said, "You might be going to stay with your Aunt Jeanne for a while."

"Why?"

He shrugged. "Because," he said.

"For how long?"

My father had finished with the topic, though, and he turned up the radio again. I didn't want to go, of course—my aunt was strongly Catholic in a way I didn't get—and I remember climbing up on the roof of our cabin when I got home, looking out at Slippery Creek, and telling myself that soon I might be living in San Antonio . . . and it was the next morning that Gary and I stopped talking as much to Rosaria on the bus. I know it sounds like there's a connection, but I don't honestly believe there was. The truth was that Rosaria kept talking all the time about running away to California or maybe Oklahoma—she had a cousin who lived in Lawton—and I grew tired of listening to it all. She made it sound like the only good thing in life was to be out on the open road, the highway whooshing past beneath you. I think that I agreed—there is always something hopeful in travel, but it is the kind of hope that sometimes borders on despair.

"You busy?" Rosaria asked two days later. She approached me at the high-school cafeteria after lunch.

"No," I said.

"You want to go for a walk?"

"Right now?"

"Yes."

"Okay."

We weren't supposed to leave the school grounds, of course, but, in any case, we slipped out the gymnasium door, crossed the playground, and headed down Baldwin Street. Rosaria wore a skirt that left her legs exposed. We walked for maybe six or seven blocks through a residential neighborhood, and then we stopped for a time at a small yellow house with a detached garage, stopped there to pet a large mongrel dog chained to a tree in the backyard. The dog barked twice, whimpered a few times, and seemed glad enough to see us. After we finished with our petting, we sat on lawn chairs on the deck not far from where the dog lay, and we shook some dangling wind chimes by the back window of the house, and then Rosaria pulled out her pack of Kools, and we blew the smoke in the air and watched it swirl up into the sky. I remember wondering what the owners of the house would say if they came home, but they never did. After a while we started feeling sorry for the dog and found a bag of dry dog food on the deck beside a spool of hose. There was a water bowl beside the dog house, but we didn't want to pour out the water so we simply lifted the bag and sprinkled its contents around the lawn. The dog went crazy with excitement, of course. Rosaria and I sat back down on the deck, squeezing into the same lawn chair, and we listened to the sounds the dog made while it was eating. I don't remember if we kissed—as strange as that might seem—but I do remember that at one point Rosaria got up and tried the side door, which turned out to be unlocked.

"Do you want to go in?" she asked.

"I don't care."

"It's open."

"Okay."

The side door took us straight into a kitchen with a rickety metal breakfast table, tan and green linoleum, an upright refrigerator, and a gas stove that didn't look like it was cleaned very often. The living room was next, and there was old carpeting and an overflowing basket of laundry on a coffee table. We kept going down a hallway past two small bathrooms, and then we went into the farthest of the three bedrooms, which had a baby crib but no baby, a narrow single bed, and a tall pine dresser painted yellow.

"It's not that bad here," Rosaria said.

"No," I said.

After that we crossed to the window to see what the dog was up to, but it turned out that we were faced the other way and all we could see was the street we'd come down in the first place, and the occasional car going by. We stood there looking out for a time, and in a funny way it didn't seem that strange to be standing at a window inside of someone else's house, looking at a yard that wasn't ours, as though we were simply living normal lives, the kind of lives that anyone might have.

ROSARIA WORKED SATURDAYS FROM nine to four at Bollinger's Dry Cleaners, but on the next Saturday she told her father she'd been asked to stay till six. I picked her up at 4:10 then drove her out to Slippery Creek, where we sat on the bank, smoked cigarettes, and watched the slow water sliding past. It was cold that day, and I put my arm around her and told her how sometimes in the summer water moccasins went swimming in the creek. "But they don't pay you any mind," I said.

"That's good," she said.

"Yes," I said.

Soon after that we started kissing, and then we lay backwards on the bank, our feet dangling toward the water. What I remember most about that afternoon is how hard the ground felt beneath us, and how cold the air felt, as though the winter winds might carry us away.

The following Saturday we avoided the creek altogether and instead went inside the cabin I shared with my father. He had gone to Minster's Tavern on Wendall Avenue, but in truth it wouldn't have made much difference. We lay on my old army blanket on my bed, watched the shadows play against the ceiling, and then got undressed. Rosaria removed her gold necklace with its tiny gold cross—out of respect for her grandmother, she said. It was cold inside the room, so Rosaria and I slipped beneath the covers and lay there with just our heads and shoulders sticking out. For a while we talked about the cold, and then Rosaria started talking again about running off to California, so I told her about a time when I was nine and my father drove us one weekend to New Orleans, Louisiana, where we ate strange food like crawfish bisque and sausage gumbo, and how we stopped one night near Lake Pontchartrain. After that I told her that I might be leaving soon for San Antonio.

She sat up very suddenly. One breast, small and dark at the tip, peeked out from the sheet and seemed to point my way.

"You are the lucky one," she said.

"I guess," I said.

"I wish it was me," she said, and then she sank back down.

THE NEXT SATURDAY MY father went to Austin to visit his ex-girlfriend. Naturally he took the pickup with him, so I had no choice but to putter around the house all day. For a time I read old magazines, and then I swept the floor and built a fire and napped some on the couch, and after that I looked again for Rosaria's necklace. She had left it on the bedside table the previous week, but by the time she'd asked about it on the bus it was no longer there or any other place that I could think of. This time I looked for maybe half an hour, but somehow it had disappeared. All week I had hoped to give it back, but now it didn't seem likely that I could. By then it was nearing five, and the darkness was closing in on the earth, so I went outside to stand for a while by Slippery Creek, put my hands in my pockets, and watched the muddy water rolling past. The river looked swollen and was moving fast. The sky was low to the earth and smelled, for some reason, like distant smoke. And that was when I saw Rosaria, out there on old Route 55, walking toward me.

I met her by the dirt path where our mailbox stood nailed atop an ancient stump. She was wearing old jeans, a Longhorns sweatshirt, and white tennis shoes. Her dark hair was tied back in a ponytail. We stopped for a moment, a cold breeze blowing down across the creek, and then she said, "My father knows about us. My sister told him everything."

"Oh," I said.

"He will be coming to find us," she said. "He'll know I'm here."

"Oh," I said again, wondering if I ought to offer to drive her home, but then I remembered that my father had the pickup.

"I'm not sure what we should do," Rosaria said.

"Me neither," I said.

In the end we went into the cabin, where the air was musty and familiar. For a while we sat on the couch, and it is possible we kissed, but what I mainly remember is that we turned on the radio to KFGN, a country music station out of Austin, and we listened to the music. Earlier my father had been paying bills—or, actually, paying only the ones we could afford—and his checkbook was on the kitchen table. At one point I stood up, put the checkbook away for him, and then brought us back two grape sodas from the refrigerator. Then, about a half hour after that, we heard her father driving up. From the window, when I peeked out, I could see Mr. Vasquez walking toward us. He was a short and stocky man, powerful through the chest, though something seemed wrong with his knees, for he walked slowly, as though he wished he didn't have to put any weight on his feet, which of course wasn't possible. When he came up the stoop I noticed that his dark hair sticking up from his head looked like the stiff bristles on a brush. He had a faraway, yet steady, look in his eyes, the way that men do when they have a certain kind of chore set before them. He reached the cabin door and knocked.

"Here he is," Rosaria said.

I stepped back once I opened the door. Mr. Vasquez surprised me, coming forward into the house so suddenly, as though his limp was lost and forgotten.

"Get to the truck, Rosaria," he said.

"You can't forbid me to see boys," she said.

"Rosaria, the truck."

"You can't run my whole life."

"Do not say another word," Mr. Vasquez said. "The truck. I mean it."

"It's embarrassing when you do things like this."

"I said go."

It wasn't until after Rosaria had left the cabin and slammed the door that Mr. Vasquez finally turned to me, edging so close we nearly touched. He had on a blue jean jacket and his heavy dark mustache was flecked with gray. There was a smell that might have been aftershave or maybe just soap, but in either case it had mixed with sweat.

"You've had your fun and now it's over," he said, his voice so quiet I had to strain to hear. He added, "Do you understand what I am saying?"

Then—and this is the part I remember best—he reached down, slipped his fingers into the front pocket of his jacket, and revealed something shiny. It was a revolver, with a two-inch blue barrel and a scuffed grip panel, not unlike the Colt my father would let me shoot at squirrels with when I was young. It looked small in his hand, but for all that I couldn't take my eyes off it. The strange part was that Mr. Vasquez didn't seem angry when he showed it to me. Instead he almost smiled, as though he thought I might appreciate the gesture. From close up he looked like a much older man than from a distance, and I saw that parts of his hair were going gray. I also noticed that his mustache curled down on the sides nearly to his chin. For a moment he held the revolver between his thumb and forefinger, half inside the pocket, half out, so I could see.

"Okay?" Mr. Vasquez asked. "Do we understand each other now?"

"Yes," I said.

"You two are too young anyway," he said. "You think about that. None of this would amount to anything anyway. Okay?"

"Okay," I said.

"Are you sure you mean it?"

"Yes."

"Because sometimes people mean something at one moment but change their minds a day or two later. This isn't like that—is it?"

"No."

"Good," Mr. Vasquez said, and he tucked the revolver back inside his pocket, turned from where we stood, and walked out of the cabin, leaving the door open as he did. I followed and watched as he climbed in the front seat, started the engine, and drove off in the truck. Dust rose into the air and then drifted off across the mesquite. Rosaria, sitting in the front seat, turned around and looked through the window toward the cabin where I was standing, her dark hair still back in a ponytail, but she didn't wave. I didn't either. I watched until the truck disappeared over the railroad tracks at Elora Ridge.

IT WAS MAYBE THREE weeks after that when I left for San Antonio. My father said I would share a room there with my cousin, attend a Catholic high school, and wear a uniform. He tried to make these facts sound interesting but couldn't. We were carrying my things out to the pickup, and I had a bad headache from drinking for one last time the night before with Gary. He lived two blocks from the Colchester County Dump, and after supper we had slipped through the wire fence and had sat drinking while looking out at all the discarded sofas, old tires, and blowing trash. I had been hoping that when I got home my father would maybe say he'd changed his mind, but, then again, I wasn't sure if it would matter, or even change a thing, not in any real or lasting sense of things.

It wasn't until my father and I were finally ready to drive off to San Antonio that I thought one last time about Rosaria. She had stopped riding the bus, and when I saw her in the hallways at school or in the cafeteria, I looked past her as though she wasn't really there. I wasn't trying to be unkind, exactly, but the truth was I couldn't remember why I liked her. Sometimes I tried, but it didn't seem to do any good, and, when I was honest, I didn't know what I would say to her in any case. When my father and I climbed into the pickup and started off, I thought of her only because she had spoken so often about getting out on the open road, about leaving everything behind, about the highway whooshing by beneath you. By then we were driving over the bridge at Slippery Creek, and I remember thinking to myself that everything about my life by that rolling water was finally over. I was wrong, of course, and indeed I returned to Slippery Creek again in early April, when my father was taken to Colchester County Hospital and died in the night of bacterial pneumonia. But in any case, it was a hopeful thought to carry me away from my father's house, and I closed my eyes inside the pickup, trying not to think any longer about Rosaria, her lost necklace, the revolver peeking out of her father's pocket, or how much I feared my life, which spread out like something unknowable before me.

Ocho Rios

I t is always at the back of Scott's mind, waiting there, informing his choices, casting shadows. He feels that if the last of the earth were somehow swept away, if there were nothing left, if even the seas dried to salt, there would still be this, his memory of his first wife in Ocho Rios. They were both in their early thirties, on their honeymoon. Their hotel-room balcony looked out on the blue Jamaican waters. What happened was a fluke, everyone said, one of those things, terrible fortune. His wife had a cerebral hemorrhage. Massive. Sudden. They were on the balcony when, without warning, she was violently sick to her stomach. She collapsed and, in short order, was no longer conscious. She died before the ambulance arrived. He remembers walking back later to the hotel, walking in the heavy Jamaican sun, and knowing that the world had altered that day, that nothing would ever return to what it had been. And even after he married again five years later, even after he had children, even after he had grandchildren, he watched each and every one of them as though their brains might suddenly fill with blood and carry them away. All of us, it seemed to him, were already ghosts. After all, the universe itself was mostly insensate— iron and stone planets, gas stars, empty molecules of space—and so it was arrogance to imagine we didn't belong that way ourselves. How could anyone truly love another person while possessing that knowledge? He'd been told often by his family he could be a cold fish. It was strange terminology, he thought. A cold fish was a dead fish, surely. They said this with love in their eyes, but whenever anyone spoke of such things, he thought at once of his first wife's eyes when they were suddenly no more alive than a doorknob or a bowling ball. And in his final moments of life, he believes, he will dream again that he is standing on that balcony with his wife in Ocho Rios, and the blue of the water will be so intense that it will almost hurt his eyes. He will have no regrets—how can a stone or a wave regret anything?—and when he is being swept off he will tell himself he is returning to some true and perfect state.

The World We Know

Once I imagined you might build a life from durable and lasting materials. It wouldn't be perfect—how could it be?—but still it would be something you could trust, something to carry you through the decades, keeping you and your family safe. I knew this couldn't be so, that the world did not construct itself like that, but still it felt as real, yet mysterious, as the scaffolding of bones inside a body.

What I remember most about the winter my son was arrested—at fifteen—is how the sky seemed to open almost every night to snow. My wife, Abby, and I would awaken each morning to gray ash drifting to the earth, gathering along the Livonia River, which was frozen in February, a white skin covering the land. Memory is not static but evolving, as changeable as the clouds, and so the snow that season—which was not particularly out of the ordinary, not for Michigan—seems to me now like something mythic, the sky trying its best to smother the open yards surrounding the houses crowding the river.

For all his life Jacob had seemed to have a room inside himself into which he stepped, closing the door behind him, pulling down the shades, and sitting there with only the company of his own thoughts. While our younger boy, Nate—he was nine that winter—spoke enthusiastically about the snow, going on and on most days about how much he hoped it would keep dropping and dropping until we all had to go sledding or maybe skiing if we wanted to travel anywhere, including to school, until we needed sled dogs and would name them Boy and Burt and Bobby and Bean and Buster, Jacob sat saying nothing at the breakfast table, sipping the Mountain Dew his mother attempted from time to time to forbid, and gazing out the window and waiting for the school bus to arrive from Morgan Heights.

"He needs friends," my wife often said.

"I know," I said.

"We should do something."

"What?"

And that was the question, of course. When Jacob was younger, Abby had made an effort to cart him from house to house to play with other boys from school, and she had encouraged mothers to send their own children over to our house, or maybe to go bowling or to the movies or roller skating. But none of it ever lasted, ever stuck. I watched the boys leaving a space between themselves and our son, making a wide berth as they moved around him. He was different, their body language said. He was not like them.

So of course we were ecstatic when he found his first girlfriend. Her name was Ruth, and she lived across the river, just beyond the gray footbridge, where the current made a sharp turn into the countryside. From our upstairs windows, we could see the wedding-cake white of their house, the slope of their backyard. Ruth was Jacob's age but attended St. Luke's instead of the public school, and she had long dark hair—the color of crow wings, I remember thinking once—and was thin nearly to the point of emaciation. She was barely over five feet and legally blind, though Jacob later informed us that she could see basic shapes and gradations of light and darkness, could even, on occasion, catch a faint inkling of color. Often she carried a white collapsible cane, and when she walked she fanned it out before her like a tentacle.

Standing beside our son, she was dwarfed. He was already almost as tall as I was, with light brown hair like his mother, often shaggy, and close-set eyes, and my overgrown Adam's apple. He was awkward in his body, awkward when he walked, awkward when he tried to speak and to gesture with his hands, and when he and Ruth were together they seemed like clay pieces that hadn't quite hardened correctly in the kiln. We didn't know how they'd met, didn't know what had drawn them to each other, didn't know how serious they were, but we did know that at long last we would hear Jacob speaking to someone late at night over the phone, and one night I saw him in the backyard, shoeless, without a coat, dressed in jeans and a soccer shirt, gazing across the river toward her house. Often we saw him walking with Ruth in the cold by the water, or she entered our home and sat with our son in the family room, their soft voices like humming insects. At night, in bed, Abby and I would marvel and whisper about such things, would assure ourselves that the phase our son had been going through since childhood was finally lifting, that the veil was rising to reveal the gentle and sensitive boy we had always known was waiting to emerge.

Jacob was arrested a few weeks later for taking Ruth's life. How can any parent imagine such a thing? I remember fishing with him and his brother when they were younger, our angled lines reaching out into the muddy waters, our bobbers afloat. I remember imagining that the current of the river was changeable in ways that displayed, somehow, a kind of sentience. The waters were green or brown by day, gray at dusk or dawn, and black at night. And always they had somewhere they needed to be, always heading out in the same direction, purposeful and serious. Occasionally we saw herons in the shallows, as still as statuary, or else the great birds lifted themselves awkwardly and made their way into the resistance of the air. And always I was glad to be there with my sons, as though love exists mostly in those quiet moments when you are saying nothing, when the wind is desultory in the leaves, when the gnats or mosquitoes are levitating around your body, when a day moon is ghostly and watching in the sky.

"I did it," Jacob told us at the Sheriff's station.

"No," Abby said. "No, you didn't."

He blinked, blinked again. "I did."

Is it possible to replay events over and over that you never actually saw, to put them on a recurring loop so that every hour of every day of your life seems tethered to them? And since memory evolves or devolves, is discursive rather than linear, is it possible to construct those events with endless minor or even major variations, to alter them and to improvise, to attempt to shade them in more palatable directions?

The basic facts are so simple you might place them on a notecard:

They were arguing on the bridge.

Ruth grabbed his coat to try to keep him from storming off.

He shoved her and she went tumbling over the railing to the frozen river.

I have worked for most of my adult life as an insurance agent in Morgan Heights, so of course I am well aware of how houses flood and trees fall and people slip off back porches and lightning burns the clothes off a body and children drown in unattended pools and dogs bite and gunfire shatters windows and people take their own lives. This is the world as we know it, and yet I have spent all these years now envisioning minor revisions to my son's history. What if the girl had fallen back against the railing on the bridge but hadn't gone over? What if she had fallen but hadn't broken her neck? What if my son had forgiven her for the fact that she had confessed to him an interest in another boy from school? What if, more reticent, she had kept that fact to herself? What if we had kept Jacob home that night so he might complete his algebra—his grade always hovered in that class near the failing mark—or it had snowed so heavily that they had decided not to meet outside but had spoken instead by phone? For decades now I have heard in my mind the ambulance siren coming closer. I was placing dishes in the dishwasher, so gazed out the kitchen window at the revolving lights, otherworldly. Soon there were police cars, too, and then I could see the beams of flashlights moving down toward the river, the commotion of bodies that appeared in the winter like dark ink smudges.

As a boy I had often wondered how prayers lifted from pews to find their way through cracks in the church ceiling, and if some fell back to earth as they were rising, catching in the limbs of trees, losing their way. And I had wondered about the ones that arrived at last at their destination. Was God overwhelmed by the number and the desperation of the pleas, all of it sounding like so many bees buzzing in a hive?

And I remember the days, then years, following the fall as a kind of extended prayer. First, of course, we could think of nothing but the hope that the girl would live, that they would save her at the hospital. Then we kept telling ourselves that surely he wouldn't be charged, that everyone would have to see that it was a horrible accident, that although the death was tragic, it would only compound the human suffering to have our sweet boy sent to a juvenile facility. Then Abby and I insisted to each other that since it would only be three years, we would all survive it, would all work through it and continue with our lives on the other side. Jacob, perhaps, would forge a bond with the boys around him—all of them outcasts now—would find that the terrible sadness of what had occurred would nonetheless be for him a turning point.

And there was our other boy, Nate, after all. Nate had to ride the bus to school each day, hear the whispers about his brother and about the blind girl tumbling through the air, endure the lies and the exaggerations and the cruelty. The girl was pregnant, one of the stories went. Jacob strangled her before throwing her to her death. Once when he was younger, Nate had turned over while he was tubing in the Livonia River, and I remembered fearing that he had struck his head, that blood would seep into the moving current. He was fine, it turned out, and Abby and I kept saying the same thing now. Our boy was fine. Both our boys were fine. We would all of us get past this. We would find that happiness was more resilient than people often imagined. We would return to a life with a firm and permanent foundation.

That was the world we knew, but it wasn't the world in which we lived. When, at eighteen, Jacob was released from the facility near Detroit, and we brought him home in the car, carried his suitcase up to his room, touched his face with our hands, kissed his cheeks, we never would have guessed that he would remain with us for less than three months before buying a bus ticket to San Diego. He didn't tell us he was leaving. He didn't say goodbye. He told Nate he was going, but Nate, by then, was so constantly in trouble at school and in his personal life that he rarely shared with us anything at all, if he could help it, except to rail at how controlling we were, how overprotective just because our other son had killed someone, just because we no longer trusted either of them. Much later we would learn that Nate had already tried heroin by then, but no parent would ever imagine such a thing, not in a boy of twelve. Jacob left us and did not write or call, and the more our younger son courted trouble, the more we feared that he—our good son—seemed destined for a life as tragic as his brother's.

That didn't happen. Nate moved to Chicago when he was nineteen, went there with a girl who was also, we later learned, an addict, but both of them lived, and we heard from them two or three times each year, still hear from them, especially now that we have two grandchildren. I would like to say that we are happy for Nate, but Abby and I have long since come to be suspicious of such things. We moved long ago from the house along the Livonia River, and live now in a crowded neighborhood in Morgan Heights, on a street where children are often laughing and on bicycles or playing jump rope. We know their parents think their lives are safe, that caution is the order of the day. And as for Jacob, we haven't heard from him in more than two decades. He went into that room he kept within himself, and threw away the key. But I think of him often, as you can imagine, and once, last winter, I drove to the old house in the snow, and I walked out onto the bridge where that poor girl—I can still picture Ruth vividly—fell to her death. And as I leaned against the railing, I watched the snow dipping and moving like frenetic moths around my body, and I told myself, as I often have over the years, that Jacob was alive somewhere, maybe with a wife and children, maybe with a decent job, and perhaps he had climbed enough from his shell that he could play with his sons and daughters, could smile and tease and tickle them, and had long ago forgiven himself for what had occurred. I want this to be so, and it seemed in that moment as the snow was everywhere around me, and the Livonia River was frozen into stasis, that it was as true as anything else in this world, and perhaps that meant it was possible.

Old Places

Kayla is watching for her cats. She expects them to slip at any moment from the woods at the edge of the backyard. She hopes it's not the orange cat, though, or the black one. Her mother tells her the cats are probably wild and riddled with cat diseases, but she likes to give the one she calls Bunches—a tiger cat—the treats her mother buys for Coco, who lives indoors and is so old and fat she sleeps most of the time in slabs of sunlight falling through the windows. Bunches will rub against your leg and make little engine sounds while she takes the treats, which are shaped like tiny stars and fish. Kayla likes to kneel down on the stoop or sidewalk or grass, count out the treats: *one, two, three, four, five.* That's how many Bunches gets. The orange cat doesn't get any. The black cat gets three.

Today Kayla has been waiting a long time. Her mother says it's no one's fault that she has no summer friends, that she spends so much time standing at the kitchen window, watching for the cats. Her mother says it's possible to be one of God's angels even if only God knows it. But none of this concerns Kayla right now. She is thinking about how she will turn twelve in less than a week, how she is growing up, even if the kids in the neighborhood still tease her, even if the kids at church make fun of her for reading from the Bible with a finger touching the words, sounding out sentences too slowly. It is frustrating, she admits, but all those feelings will go away once Bunches begins sitting in her lap. What she feels for the animal is something no book could ever express, no matter, even, if God wrote it.

Kayla's family moved from Kentucky to Ohio when she was nine, and the little town where they live is called Wallace Heights. But it's not actually high above the ground—it's flat, especially the road the school bus takes. She does know that there are barns at the nearby houses that supposedly have what her mother says are wild cats, though Kayla has always found them to be friendly, always coming to her backyard to swirl around her legs.

It is Bunches that arrives finally this morning—not from the woods but from the direction of the driveway. Kayla runs out the back door. One night she dreamed the cat was high in a tree in the oldest part of the woods, calling out in distress, so Kayla began climbing and climbing up the bark. She planned to carry the cat back down to safety, but then, in the dream, she was up in the bright leaves while the cat was back on the ground. It almost seemed, then, that she was the cat instead of Bunches. She began crying or maybe mewling in the dream, and when she woke she was somehow crying in the world, crying with love because her lungs couldn't manage to hold it in.

Bunches is still coming toward her across the driveway when the Behn brothers—Todd and Marcus—run out from the hedges next door with long sticks. The sticks slap at the driveway, slap at the cat, make a racket like what Kayla's mother would call trying to wake the dead. The brothers, her next-door neighbors, are ten and nine, and the cat makes a strange moan as the sticks create their commotion around it. Then the cat is low-slung and skittering into the undergrowth, and both brothers throw their sticks to follow it.

"Stop!" Kayla screams.

The boys carry their startled expressions with them as they pivot to face her.

"Don't hurt Bunches!" she cries out.

For one fraction of a moment the brothers appear stunned— but then the older boy, Todd, recovers. "We're not going to hurt it," he says. "We're going to kill it."

"Smash in its head," Marcus adds.

"Put a fish hook through its lip and dangle it from a tree," Todd says.

"Stop it!" Kayla says.

"Throw it in the river and use it for bait," Marcus says.

"And maybe use you for bait, too," Todd says. "Throw you in the river beside it."

Kayla is roaring inside herself by then, roaring toward the back door to escape, letting the screen door slam behind her, letting the words of the boys fill the air like the terrible and acrid summer dust that lifts from the county road sometimes in dry weather, that wants to choke her lungs.

THERE'S A HISTORY HERE, after all. Kayla thinks of it sometimes as like pointing a magnifying glass at dead leaves until finally one catches fire. She saw that happen once in the playground at school. She saw the leaf curl and darken, then transform into an orange, licking tongue. Then she watched the leaf disappear down to nothing. All the anger of her life is focused sometimes on the Behn brothers. She hates them beyond hate, a little island of fury all by itself, where nothing exists beyond how much she wishes them damage.

Once, the previous summer, she tattled on them for setting off cherry bombs and M-80s in the woods behind her house, blowing up rotting logs and even an old bird house they must have stolen. She watched them from the verge of the woods, then told her mother, who told their mother, who punished them. The brothers then called Kayla a fat retard for the telling, so she hated them even more, hated them as much as she loved Bunches, as though the cat and the brothers were opposite poles of each other, two worlds that somehow needed each other for reasons Kayla only dimly understood. What she did know for certain was that come winter the boys threw snowballs at her while she was waiting for the bus, so she told her mother, who told their mother, who punished them, so the boys threatened to soak her in gasoline and set her on fire with a lighter if she ever told on them again, so she told her mother, who told their mother, who punished her sons once more. The brothers finally told everyone at school that Kayla still had to wear diapers because she was too stupid and too much a baby not to have an accident, which wasn't true, though no one believed it.

Now, though, things are even worse. The Behn brothers, after all, know what she loves, which violates the first and only rule of getting by: *don't let them know anything.* She blames herself, of course. If she'd simply said nothing, had simply retreated back into the house, Bunches would have run off safely, and the Behn brothers would have been none the wiser. But now, because she is as stupid as people always say she is, because she didn't think before she acted—which is something her mother always reminds her—she is lost. Her words formed from some primitive need inside her body, something ancient, and they were so old and powerful she couldn't stop them from making their way into the world.

So what more is there to do? She watches each day at the window, watches for the cats. And when she sees the orange cat, she does her best to disguise her loathing. She feeds it for the first time ever, dropping the fish- and star-shaped treats onto the grass, watching the cat she despises come forward for the reward. And when she sees the black cat, she feeds it, but only a little before shooing it away. And when she sees Bunches, when her heart grows swollen like fruit that sags the limb of a tree with its weight, she shoos it away. Yells at it. Says terrible things about how ugly it is, how much she can't stand the sight of it. And Bunches is confused, of course. Bunches keeps trying to come toward her, trying to swirl around her legs, trying to climb into her lap. Bunches gives a small cry of hunger from its belly. Bunches wants the tuna she gave it once from a tin she found at the back of her mother's cupboard, the stinky fish smell that is heaven, wants to lap up the juice and take the flakes of it into its mouth, chew them down as an offering. Kayla keeps wanting to rub her hand down the cat's back and up the little rope of its tail, but she imagines the Behn brothers coming back with their sticks or worse, watching from behind the hedges, watching from the windows of their brick house, watching because that's the evil they do and the evil they are.

"Get," she says to Bunches. "Get!"

The cat backs off, then comes forward again.

"Get!" Kayla moans.

ON SUNDAY THE BOYS bring her a kitchen wastebasket, carrying it from their side of the hedges. She is in the backyard, feeding the orange cat. It is the warmest day yet of the summer, and she is dressed in shorts and a T-shirt. The T-shirt has a cat and a ball of yarn on the front of it. The sprinkler is on and arcing one way, then the next, and the orange cat is letting her pat its head as it rubs against her. She looks up and the brothers are coming toward her, carrying the plastic wastebasket. She knows this can't be good. The boys are looking pleased with themselves, which is very, very bad. The orange cat runs off as the boys approach, so desperate to be gone that it runs straight through the water of the sprinkler. The cat knows. *Knows.*

The older brother, Todd, says, "Is your mother home?"

"Go away," Kayla says.

"Answer the question, Kaka," Todd says.

"Yes, she is," Kayla says.

"No, she's not," Marcus says. "You're too stupid to know how to lie. The car isn't in the driveway, Kaka."

"She'll be back soon," Kayla says.

"Do you want to know what we've got here?" Todd asks.

"Go away—I'll tell on you," Kayla says.

"Look," Todd says, and he lifts the lid. At first she fears it will be the tiger cat, will be Bunches. She knows that what she will feel will be like a painting she saw once in a book of a man with his body full of arrows. He was supposed to be a saint, but all she saw were the barbs making mayhem of his body, existing both inside and outside his flesh. She knows she will not survive this. But it's not Bunches—it's the black cat. At first she knows it must be dead, but then it starts to scramble to lift itself, to climb free, its eyes wide with exaggerated, cartoon terror. She can hear the sounds of it shuffling and scrambling and scratching, hear the sounds like something hidden away and primitive, hear the sounds she can't bear. And there is a bright red smear of blood on one corner of the green plastic, a badge of it she can't stop studying, can't turn away from. Then Todd slams down the top again, holds it tight, and the cat makes a sound like something thrown up out of the center of its body, something sorrowful and desperate, something she knows, even then, she will never forget.

"Let the cat go," she says, unable to stop herself.

"No," Todd says.

"No," Marcus says.

"We're going to kill it," Todd says. "We wanted to show you first. Wanted you to know."

"This is what happens when you tattle," Marcus says.

"We're going to hang it," Todd says. "We're going to put a noose around its neck and hang it from a branch in the woods."

"We're going to make you watch," Marcus says.

"I'll tell," Kayla says.

"No you won't," Todd says.

"I'll tell my mother," Kayla says. "You know I will."

"Then we'll hang you from a tree," Todd says.

"My mother will tell your mother," Kayla says. "You'll be in trouble."

"We'll hang you right beside your stupid cat," Marcus says.

"You'll both be dead," Todd says.

"I don't care," Kayla says. "I'll tell. I will. Don't think I won't."

Then the brothers are looking back and forth between her and each other. And the cat is crying inside its enclosure, something so deep and ancient in its body that it is almost impossible for Kayla to listen to. And though she knows it's not Bunches there, knows Bunches is somewhere else and safe, she keeps imagining that the crying belongs to Bunches, too, if that is possible.

"The only way I won't tell is if you let the cat go," Kayla says.

The boys look at each other. Then they look at the plastic garbage bin enclosing the cat. She can feel them hesitate, the way you can feel the earth spin around you when you grow dizzy.

"We're going to kill it," Todd says. "Then bury it. No one will ever see it again."

"I'll tell," Kayla says.

"We'll say we let it go," Todd says.

"My mother will tell your mother," Kayla says.

"The cat will still be dead," Todd says. "We'll bury it alive."

Then they are carrying the cat away from her, carrying it in what Kayla will later imagine is its plastic coffin, carrying it back to the hedges and their yard and away, carrying it out of her life forever, carrying it to where she knows she will never see it again. And there is nothing to be done but to go inside, to stand at the living-room window and watch for her mother to return, to wait for her mother. There is nothing to be done but to remember the sounds the cat made from deep inside its body, to harden herself to the orange cat and to Bunches, especially to Bunches, to hate the cats as much as she hates the Behn brothers, to despise the cats each time she sees them out the window, out in the yard coming from the woods, to never feed them, not even once. And as soon as her mother is home, she knows, as soon as she has told on Todd and Marcus, she will strip off her T-shirt and throw it in the trash, will put on a different one, will never feed Bunches again or want to, never hear Bunches purr beneath the stroking of her hand, never give Bunches a treat. She will tell the Behn brothers she doesn't care if they kill them all, torture them all, skin them and wear them as hats. She doesn't care about any of it or anything, and not just to keep the cats safe, not just because she wants them away from her yard, but because it is true, because she will stop feeling anything every time Bunches comes toward her, will stop feeling anything at all when people ask why she has no friends or tell her how stupid she is.

Folklore

The boy believes his father is a bear. He learned in school that bears hibernate in winter, closing themselves up in their dens for as much as eight long months. The boy's father doesn't have a den but does have a study, right next to the bedroom the boy shares with his older brother. The study has a desk in it, a couch, a bed. Their father closes himself up in that room when he doesn't want to be disturbed. That's what their mother says, at least. *Play quietly. Don't disturb your father.* And what does their father do when he is hibernating? Sometimes he is in there with his headaches. Only later will the boy learn that they are migraines, that they burrow like that bear in its den, but in this case the den is beneath the father's left eye, which throbs so that sometimes he is actually sick to his stomach and can't abide any light, and the softest sounds are more than he can handle. But other times the boy's father is in there with his *moods.* When his mother says that word, both the boy and his brother know it is time to be careful. They learn to watch their father's hands. Once the boy bled from his nose so badly onto the kitchen floor that his mother needed a bucket and a mop. Another time the boy saw his father with his hands around his mother's neck the way a bear might engulf you in its great arms. There was a fact the boy learned in school: if a bear comes into your camp, if you are asleep in your tent and the bear is there looking for food, you are supposed to bang together pots and pans. Bears don't like loud sounds, it seems. But that's not the way things are with his father. With his father, the boy has learned to walk quietly past the closed study door, to keep his voice so soft that not even his mother or his brother can hear him. That doesn't mean the boy doesn't like it when his father lets him sit in his lap. Of course he does. Their father tells the story of living as a child in Michigan with his family, how there were bears you could feed at garbage dumps. The bears would practically take the food from your hands, their father said. The boy loves his father when he thinks about that story, loves how his father would save scraps from his supper to offer to the bears. His father also tells the story of a bear he saw once while vacationing in Wisconsin. The bear had a chain around its neck and drank grape or orange soda. You could buy it in a bottle and the bear would lift it in two paws, then drink. The boy thinks about this sometimes when he is sitting in his father's lap or riding on his father's shoulders. His father once shared a grape soda with a bear, taking a few sips himself, then giving the rest to the giant beast. And sometimes the boy dreams his father is that bear with the chain around his neck, or that bear begging for food at the garbage dump, or maybe just a bear asleep in its den. The boy imagines that last one the most—especially after his father is gone from their lives. By then the study door on the second floor of the house is always open. By then the desk is empty of papers. His father was an accountant in their small Ohio town, but no longer. Now their father isn't anything at all. He's like the bear that forgets to come out of its den when winter passes, when the grass grows and the air drifts warm and humid. His father is now dreaming of snow, perhaps, or so the boy likes to imagine. His father is snug inside his den while the earth turns to ice. It was the boy's older brother who found their father with his head down on his study desk, the pistol beside him. Only much later did the boy learn that his father placed the tip of that barrel inside his mouth—the way, as a boy, he had placed the glass bottle in his mouth before handing it over to the bear. But the boy, even when he is older, doesn't like to think about that. His father wasn't a fat man, after all, and in that way he hadn't seemed like a bear, but he had seemed large to the boy, and sometimes after he drank his bourbon the air in his study would seem dense and rancid, the way you might imagine a bear's den might smell. And when the boy is older still, when he is an adult and begins having migraines behind his own left eye, when he needs to be alone sometimes from his own wife and his children, he will think about his father, will imagine him closed up inside his study. And he will try to formulate what a bear must dream about inside its den during a long and desolate winter, how the world must seem so much a cold and endless dream. The boy will imagine climbing into that den and closing out the world, having only his own suffering to keep him company, only his father to keep him company—with no one there to hand either of them grape soda in a bottle.

Five Grackles

George has always known. Always. It is there like the creek in the woods behind the house, a thing that dries to nothing sometimes, is swollen others, but always there, no matter what, no matter that you often wished it were somewhere else.

His brother's name is Curt, short for Curtis. At nine, Curt is one year younger than George. And once when George spotted a coyote trotting out of the woods, coming from the direction of the soybean field that belonged to the neighbor, he thought at once of his brother. The creature was low-slung and wild. And another time, in winter, George found drops of blood on the snow in the open field beyond the fence, though blood from what he never knew. Once again it was Curt that came to mind.

The truth is there are so many signs to contend with, so many complications and bad occurrences. It is early spring now, and he and his brother are throwing dirt balls and rocks at one another. It is Sunday, and they are not long back from church. They have changed from their good clothes. George is running into the woods, carrying the top of a plastic garbage can for a shield. His brother is coming after him, and it is dangerous, very, because Curt got hit in his leg with a rock George threw. So George climbs across where the fence has been bent on its back from a fallen tree. He climbs across the dead tree to get into the soggy field. And he is running, now, through wet mud. The mud makes sucking sounds.

"Stop chasing me," George says to his brother while he is coming after him over the fence. "Stop."

"I'm going to break open your skull," Curt calls.

"Stop," George says.

"I'll stop when your brains are leaking out," Curt says.

So George runs. The house where they live with their parents is surrounded by fields and rural roads, and far-away and scarce neighbors, so there is no escape. And his brother, behind him, is carrying a rock as large as a fist. George hears his own breaths making their way into the air, escaping into air, but he knows he will never get away. He hears his brother's footsteps in the mud of the field, hears the wind rushing out from the west, blowing across them like something mindless. The wind wants to knock them from their feet, and Curt wants to knock George from his feet with the rock, and his side feels like a knife is stabbing against his ribs from so much running. Finally he stops, turns, and faces what he knows he must face.

"You can't have one that big," he calls out to his brother.

"Your head will crack open like an egg," Curt says.

"It's not funny," George says.

Then Curt is nearly upon him, and George holds the green plastic shield before his body for protection, holds it out in supplication. His brother is stepping toward him through what, at this far edge of the field, is tall grass. And then something remarkable happens. Just as Curt is raising the rock, something dark flies up from the ground. There is a frantic shudder of wings. Later George will think the bird was a grackle, but he doesn't know for sure. All dark birds, to him, are grackles . . . unless they are enormous enough to be crows. And so the grackle flies up and makes what might be a squawking sound or might be a frantic coo. Whatever it is, it sounds older to George than the mud itself, older than the sky. And the bird, in its effort to be free, flies the wrong direction, flies directly into Curt's chest, striking him there, battering him, as though trying to fly through his flesh and into his body, to become him.

Then it is flying off, and Curt has dropped the rock and is punching George instead, hitting him on his arm and chest, hitting him over and over, and all George can think about is that grackle that flew straight into his brother, and how his brother barely seemed to notice or care, how, to his brother, a bird trying to burrow through your skin and perch forever on your ribs was an ordinary occurrence. George ducks into the blows, feeling them storm against him, feeling the pain like something ripped from you. Then it is done. Curt is winded and is sitting on the mud of the field.

"Let's go ride bikes," Curt says after a moment.

"You're an asshole," George says.

"We can ride to the quarry."

"You hurt my arm."

"We'll race there."

"I don't want to," George says.

"What do you want to do then?" Curt asks.

GEORGE IS DESPERATE AFTER that. Of course he is. Even more so than usual. Soon it is summer and he doesn't even have school as a place to find time away from his brother. He's never liked school particularly, but now he dreams of sitting at his homeroom desk while Mrs. Gates rattles on, dreams of how he might walk the hallways or sit at a table in the lunchroom without someone shooting rubber bands at his head or throwing his clothes out the window or tripping him when he walks. At home he tries to avoid Curt by watching TV or reading a comic, but then their mother shoos them outside, and that's that. One day, for example, Curt soaks him with the hose, then knocks him down and sits on him. George struggles to be free, and while he does he notices something he can't explain. A smell. It's Curt's skin or maybe his hair or his clothes. He smells like something rotting on the surface of a stagnant pond when it turns green. He smells like when their father discovered a dead mouse behind the furnace in the basement. He smells like something that lives in the woods or under a rock or comes from some distant land where people wear animal skins instead of clothes.

"Get off," George says.

"You wet your pants," Curt says.

"Get off," George says. "You stink."

And in a dream that night Curt is sitting on him once again, though in the dream they must be near the patio because their mother's flower pots are all around them, one of them broken and overturned, and George keeps staring at the broken pot and worrying that his brother will lift one of the sharp shards and slice his throat. And when George looks up, he sees that his brother now has the body and head of a bird. And it occurs to him that maybe it is the same bird that flew into his brother's chest to live there. Then Curt is trying to peck at his eyes with his sharp beak, and the beak is hammering against George's face, and he feels the ice pick of the beak burrow into the soft egg of his eye . . . and he is awake, now, breathless, climbing from the lower bunk to stand at the window. And he can hear Curt breathing loudly from the upper bunk, breathing like some wild creature in its lair, and George has the sudden impulse to smother Curt with a pillow, to make the breathing stop, but then he pictures his brother gouging out his eyeballs with his fingers and placing the bloody orbs on the floor to stamp on them with his bare feet. George leans his hands against the window sill and looks out at the skull of moon where it is buried in the sky's mud.

HIS BROTHER, TODAY, IS carrying the .22. It belongs to their father. You load the rifle bullets one by one. You pull back the bolt to expose the chamber. You slip the bullet into the slot. You close the bolt. You aim and pull the trigger, hearing the small explosion, feeling the little kick. You open the bolt and the empty shell casing goes flying. Usually, the boys shoot only with their father, but today their father and mother have gone to visit Aunt Dory. Their parents might be as far away as the sun. And Curt knows where their father hides the key to the lock on the rifle, knows where the bullets are hidden high in the bedroom closet shelf. So now they are hunting in the woods behind their house. Curt shoots twice at squirrels high up on limbs, and George shoots once, and the squirrels twitch their tails but never fall. The squirrels have special powers, it seems, and so the boys take turns shooting at Coke cans they place atop a fallen log, but they can't seem to hit them either unless they stand too close to make it fair. Then there is a dark bird atop the wire fence at the edge of the woods, and Curt aims quickly and fires. At once there is a confetti of feathers in the air, as though the bird has shattered into pieces, as though the bird was as brittle as hardened clay. Then the boys are running toward the bird, and they find it on the ground near the fence, there amid some purple wildflowers. They poke the black bird with a stick, and the bird doesn't move, and Curt touches the bird with his bare finger but George refuses.

Then Curt says, "Run."

"What?" George says.

"Run. I'll count to five."

And Curt is pointing the rifle at him, and George is running, thrashing through the woods, and Curt is counting out the numbers loudly, shouting them to exist in the air, to reverberate through the sky. George imagines the bullet forcing its way through his flesh, the way the bird tried to force its way into his brother, then Curt yells "five," and George ducks behind a tree. He hears his brother laughing hysterically, so he peers out and sees Curt walking toward him, the rifle perched harmlessly on his shoulder—the way a marching soldier might carry it. His brother comes up beside him and is carrying the dead bird in his free hand, the limp neck dangling.

"You moron," Curt says.

"That wasn't funny," George says.

"I bet you shit yourself," Curt says.

THEY RIDE THEIR BIKES to the quarry. It is made of limestone. There are steep walls and far drops. There is green water at the bottom, like a lake without waves, a motionless eye gazing up at you. The open hole in the earth makes George think of a tooth gone from a mouth, or a deep grave where some ancient beast was once buried but then unearthed. There is a high fence around the property and "No Trespassing" signs, but the boys know a tear in the back of the fence, an opening large enough to get their bikes through. And the boys know that the place is almost always deserted, that they can throw rocks from the top and watch them arc the long way down until they splash in the quiet world below, making a commotion that is strangely gratifying. And the boys know they can spit off the side of the high cliff, or urinate, and watch the liquids from their bodies combine with the green liquid at the bottom, becoming one. The boys step off their bikes and walk to the edge of the quarry, peer down. It is dizzying how far a drop it is, mesmerizing.

"Don't fall," Curt says, giving his brother a pretend little shove.

"Stop it," George says.

"You're such a baby," Curt says.

"I mean it," George says.

Then Curt is grabbing him by the waist and trying to push him toward the edge, and the edge keeps coming nearer, and George grips tightly to his brother so they both will fall, if it comes to that. And George keeps thinking about a story he once heard about a boy who supposedly tried to jump from the top of the quarry into the water, who broke his neck and died, though he isn't certain it is true. He heard the boy was trying to impress a girl, that they'd just had sex with their clothes off at the top of the quarry, that the boy had jumped naked and had died naked, was hauled away forever without his clothes on. And George thinks about falling in the open air, and he imagines his brother letting loose and turning into a black bird, the same one from the dream, and flying off to safety, maybe squawking.

"You're an ass," George says, but then his brother lets go and they ride their bikes down the narrow path at the far side of the quarry, down and down until they can get off their bikes at the water's edge. They strip down to their shorts—both of them are wearing cut-off jeans—and wade into the water. It is always colder than George expects, like something from another world, a place where there is snow and ice instead of summer. They swim out toward the center, and from there the cliffs look like the great wall of a prison, or some ancient monument built by a distant tribe that once ruled the world and made blood sacrifices to their hungry gods.

And they swim until they are exhausted, and after that they sit by the water's edge and talk about boys and girls and teachers from their school they would most like to drown, would like to hold underneath the water at the quarry until they stopped kicking and lay still. Then the bodies would float out across the still waters, face down, or maybe even sink to the bottom, never to be seen again.

"What about Charlie Levin?" Curt says.

"We'll drown him, too," George says.

"Good," Curt says. "He's a good one to drown."

Then, without warning, Curt is tackling George and pushing him into the water, saying his brother ought to be drowned, come to think of it, that surely they shouldn't leave him out, that he deserves to be drowned as much as anyone. And then George loses his balances and is underwater, is swallowing water, and it tastes like mud or maybe worse, and he feels his brother trying to hold him underneath the surface, imagines dying there and sinking to the bottom, looking up with dead eyes to the faint light of a sun he'll never see again, the last of his life trailing away until he isn't certain any longer if he is any more alive than the limestone or the water itself or the fence with the rip down its belly. He knows he is dying, but then a miracle occurs, something astonishing. He bobs up in the water and is free, is gasping for air, is alive again. But his brother, Curt, who has been trying to murder him, has lost his balance or his footing and has slipped beneath the surface himself, and George places both hands on his brother's shoulders and tries to hold him there for all eternity. And his brother begins thrashing like that Jensen girl at school with epilepsy—someone else they added to their drowning list—thrashing like a neighbor cat Curt once tried to catch with his bare hands. George holds his brother, holds him, leaning close into his brother's body. He has a vision, suddenly, of his brother sinking to the bottom instead of him, of having the bedroom to himself back home, of not having to fear his brother putting dog shit in his lunch box or tripping him down the stairs. He envisions walking out into the woods behind the house by himself, playing by himself—whatever game he wants. And so he holds his brother more and more tightly, pushing down. And he is happy now, except that the vision begins slowly to change. He imagines his brother gone—yes—but then he imagines his brother turning into the birds in the back woods and field, becoming one terrible black bird. He envisions that bird and others swooping down at him and trying to fly into his chest, or pecking at the last of his eyeballs, popping them like green grapes. It is more than he can bear—the vision—and though it's the last thing he wants, the one thing he's sure he doesn't want, he lets go of his brother, releases him entirely, climbs back on the bank and sits there, dripping.

A moment later his brother is climbing up beside him, his chest heaving. And his brother is trying to talk but can't.

"You asshole," Curt finally says. "You total asshole."

Now George keeps wishing he had drowned his brother after all. His life will never be the same. His brother will be lying in wait, will never forget this. George knows that something terrible is coming, something worse than he could ever imagine, and the only thing that's certain is that there's no escaping it.

Old Man

It seemed, sometimes, that his wife was a puff of smoke. The sort you saw rising from a chimney as you drove past.

Her clothes still waited in various closets. He was supposed to pack them into boxes for the attic or to give them away, but it hadn't happened. The drawers in the bathroom still held her pills and deodorant and hair brushes.

In the backyard was a green bench by a shagbark hickory where he sat mornings and read the newspaper. At night he drank beer there. Now, as he rolled the bottle in his fingers, it was nearly ten, fully dark. Sitting there, it seemed, was now his life. He touched the bottle to his lips and felt the liquid escape into his body—a deep well. The hours plowed the sky with stars.

The back screen door made a small sound as it bounced closed behind him, and he headed off to bed. He was retired now. He thought of this stage of life as like living all alone on a great hill overlooking a distant bustling village. Everyone down there was hurrying somewhere, had someplace to be. Voices lifted their chaos into air.

So what did he have, this high up on the hill?

Before climbing into bed, he pulled back the curtains and looked toward the limestone house next door. The neighbors were four weeks new. Renters. Two brothers, one wife . . . though which one she was wife to he couldn't say.

Music rose like the sound of cats in heat. He could feel the vibration on the glass, a living thing.

Days passed. There was hardly any moon some nights when he heard the voices of the neighbors. Always they were shouting in the dark, laughing. Mornings there was nothing there: even the dog, a scraggly German shepherd chained forever in the yard and doing its solitary penance, was silent.

Come winter, snow fell on the disabled brother as he made his way in late afternoon to the mailbox. He couldn't hold a conversation. He trembled as he spoke, his mouth too loose for words.

The other brother was called Plaid, whatever kind of name or nickname that was. Home from Iraq. One day in February they had a brief conversation in the yard, and Plaid explained that it made no sense that he didn't have a single scratch from the war, while his brother had almost died back home, in a car accident. Plaid had a tattoo on his arm that might have been a crow, a bear, or maybe a dragon.

The wife, overweight, spoke—when she talked at all—like leaves on fire. She said words all at once or simply stared at you.

Not one of them had a job. Cars, vans, and pickups were always pulling into the gravel driveway. Sometimes a half dozen at once. Parking on the grass. Often on *his* grass.

Then it was June again. The days were waves eroding the shore. It was dusk and he was sitting in a sweater on the bench. Always cold now, even in summer. Growing old meant the sun receded farther away into the sky.

He saw one night the wife opening a window and reaching out a packet of something. A man with a ponytail was standing in the driveway. He had handed over something folded in a palm.

Summers were feral now, grass growing wild across a field, without anything to hold it back. Wine bottles were thrown from next door into his yard. Red Bull cans. And once, curled like a snake that had shed its translucent skin, a condom.

He took now, nightly, to being on patrol. Walked the narrow line between the properties. In one fantasy he had the three of them kneeling on the driveway, hands behind their heads, the police on the way. In another he sat Plaid down on the green bench, explained veteran to veteran how a man behaves.

The disabled one, in real life, was carted away one early morning in an ambulance. The siren cut through air like a field thresher.

Then, in October, the brother was back again in the yard with his cane. Tapping it like a door loose on its hinges in the wind. The wife—whichever wife she was—was pregnant now, or maybe she'd been pregnant all along.

The property ran from the power line by the front curb to the narrow path leading back into the woods. He put one foot in front of the other. He carried his beer bottle in one hand. In his jacket pocket was a Springfield Sub-Compact.

It fit like a small bird in the palm.

He walked. Somehow, then, it was winter again. Snow fell out of a harvested sky. Hours drifted past like smoke. In one dream he woke to the recoil tug of the gun and saw the disabled man writhing on the grass like a catfish dragged from the water. In another, he felt the metallic bitterness against his tongue.

There was smoke in the air. He didn't know where winter had gone, where summer had gone. The leaves must have fallen from the trees. Leaf smoke drifted from a distant yard. He sat on his bench and watched the earth around him going dark. The beer bottle felt cool in his grip. The Springfield waited, primitive, inside his pocket.

Someone next door was arguing, the words beyond any meaning. There was smoke in the air. It was drifting away to where no one would ever find it.

In the spring he went to visit his daughter and her husband in California, and he stood on a beach and watched the ocean waves with their endless persistence, the water more green than blue, and inside the waves, like a strange game of peek-a-boo, he could sometimes see the outlines of fish.

He returned home to see a dozen strange cars parked along the curb and up on the grass of the house next door. He stood in the yard and heard music with a throbbing stab emerging from the open windows of the low-slung house. He found his Springfield where he'd left it in his bedroom sock drawer and tucked it into the pocket of his jacket. He walked over to the house and knocked on the front door, which was sorely in need of a coat of paint. It looked as bedraggled as the grass in the yard, which always, in the summer, appeared brown and scraggly, though too long.

The fat woman answered, her fat baby in her arms. The baby was crying, and the music was crying from the house behind them, wailing and somehow blind, a great wall of it pushing toward him.

"Can you turn down the music?" he asked.

"What?"

"The music is too loud. Turn it down."

She gave him an apoplectic look. It was a look accompanied by the increased wailing of the child, a certain flushed redness in both of their faces. There was a smell wafting out of the house, something stale and unseemly, something rotting and turning slowly to vinegar.

"Go to hell," she said. "Go to god-damn hell. My father died three days ago. We buried him this morning. I promised we'd have a party for him after he was gone, to honor him. So go to god-damn hell."

The door slammed shut, seemingly of its own volition. He didn't see her hand reach out to thrust it closed, but surely it must have, for the door had a force that rattled through his body. He walked back to the house, fingering the Springfield in his pocket. He didn't go inside. He stepped into the toolshed and found his best shovel, carried it into the woods, and buried the gun deep in the soft earth. Then he went inside and opened the door to his wife's closet. He hadn't removed a single item of her clothing. When he died, he figured, the whole house could be emptied out at once, washed away like one of those California waves coming toward you. He sat down amid the sea of his wife's shoes. For a moment he thought he might start to weep, but instead he just sat there, his wife's clothes dangling their remembrance around him.

Bedtime Story

Sometimes the two memories grow conflated in her thoughts, especially in her dreams. There is the boy she lost, who seems often like the sound of distant crows from the woods at first gray light, or like the fog that clings to the surface of the river beyond the fence. And there is the one who exists beyond her bedroom wall, who is irritable in the mornings, rubbing his eyes with the impatient backs of his hands, growing fidgety when she tries to read to him from *Charlotte's Web*. This boy throws tantrums when he is denied a piece of chocolate cream pie for breakfast or is punished for pulling the dog's tail, and he lies on his stomach and laughs at the explosions and mayhem of his cartoons. The other son is the sound of the insects speaking in tongues to the moon still adrift above the trees. Often, when she can, she walks down to the river, leaving her husband and her son to fend for themselves, and she lets the mosquitoes anoint her skin in blood, and she sits on the bank to watch the passage of the muddy water. Her first son died in the sixth month of the pregnancy, though mainly what she recalls are the dark stains of blood on her pants and undergarments when she returned from the hospital—the clothes in a plastic bag—and she has a distant memory of her father sometimes hunting for squirrels when she was a child, how the creatures, when they were shot, fell from the high limbs and struck the earth with an audible thump. And she remembers how, in winter, she saw the blood from those squirrels on the white snow, and how her mother would skin the animals, then stew the meat with potatoes and corn kernels and tomatoes. And always, of course, she carries the memory of childhood with her back to the house and to her son, who slaps at her with his little hands if he doesn't get what he wants, and wants *now*. Her dead son, though, is the slant of the sunlight through the windows, the stillness of the dust motes becalmed in the air, the breath of August wind seeping through the screen mesh. Still, as she stands cooking at the stove and seeing her son slapping a hand pointlessly against the table, she reminds herself how sometimes at night when he falls asleep in her lap, when she feels the weight of him against her, when she touches her lips to the top of his head, there is a boy smell to his body that seems to her like every son.

Into the Woods

Henry wonders if he is making a mistake, if he should head back, if his father has gotten home from work yet. But mostly he thinks about the tracks in the shallow snow as he climbs up from the creek into the denser part of the woods. Steps over a fallen log that is rotting at its center and spilling itself onto the white powder. Sees more crescent moons, a cluster of them, all in the same area again, as though the deer are milling about. He moves quietly toward what appears to be the end of the woods, what appears to be a wire fence. Walks in the direction of an open patch of field, the dead grass brown and swaying in the January wind. He is not certain how far from home he has strayed, but he is certain about the Marlin 30-30 in his hands, the heft of it as he moves up from the bottomlands. In a dream the night before, he imagined firing the rifle at the moon, knocking away chips of the great orb, until it sank bloodied and maimed to the earth, where he climbed atop it. Now the nagging voice in his head reminds him that his father has never let him hold the gun except in his presence, that his father would say he isn't old enough to wander off into woods with a rifle, but Henry doesn't care. He listens to the sound of his boot steps. Tries to move quietly, tries not to let the snow crunch or the twigs snap. Tries to be invisible in the woods, to move as a ghost might move. The rifle feels strangely warm in his bare hands, which makes no sense—the rest of him is cold. His exposed ears are burning ice.

He sees the deer out of the corner of his eye. Five of them. No, six. In the field. All statue still and gazing in the opposite direction of where he stands. He lifts the rifle and looks through the scope. Looks for antlers but isn't certain he sees any. At least not any large ones. Not like the buck's head his father keeps on the basement wall, the deer looking at him with its dark glassy eyes. These deer are so near there is no possibility of missing them if he shoots. But there are trees in the way. One in particular has dropped dozens of strange green balls onto the snow. Some animal—perhaps raccoons—have eaten the fruit and left the green bits scattered. Henry wants to move closer to the fence to get a cleaner shot, but he is worried about stepping on the green balls, making a sound that will make the deer aware that he is there. His breath rises out of his mouth in an expectant cloud. He watches the deer with their heads raised and ears up, looking in the wrong direction.

Then they are running. It happens so quickly he doesn't have the chance to shoot. The strange thing is they are running toward him, running toward the fence, and then one after another they leap into the air. First the front legs go over and then the back. They lift their large bodies in a way that seems otherworldly, and this makes him want even more to shoot them, to bring them back to earth, to catch them in mid-flight. When they leap he sees their white underbellies, as white as the snow that has fallen to the ground, as white as the tooth of moon that has lifted itself in late daylight at the field's edge. He aims the rifle, but the truth is that the deer are coming straight toward him, racing through the woods, the sounds of their hooves and their bodies a loud stampede. For a moment he envisions them trampling him or leaping over him. He fumbles for the trigger, but then the deer see him and shift directions, like a school of spooked fish. Most head to his right, making a sharp turn to fly through the woods, but one remaining deer, a doe, runs directly across his path to his left, parallel to the fence. He points the rifle without aiming and pulls the trigger. Feels the familiar recoil against his shoulder, hears the sound of the shot reverberating through the woods, as loud as thunder striking a tree. Birds squawk out of an oak not far from the fence, their wings flapping like dark scraps of sky. He works the lever to pump another bullet into position, and he recalls the sight of the bullet casing flying out into the snow beside one of the green balls. But mostly he watches the doe. She stumbles as the gun goes off, as though the loudness of the sound causes her back legs to buckle. The deer emits a deep expelled breath, something forced from her lungs. But still she keeps running. Parallel to the fence. Weaving through the trees. He sees her leap a fallen log, sees the flash of her belly. Henry realizes he is running, too. Running in the direction of the wounded deer.

Chasing it. Not caring now how much noise he makes. Running blindly along the fence line, then away from the fence as the deer moves back toward the interior of the woods. Running toward the creek, which in summer winds through the woods but now is frozen and slick. Running through a strange clearing in the woods, an open patch where there is only grass and a small hill, the dull, dusk sunlight falling against him. The light doesn't feel warm against his body. He is breathing loudly from the exertion, and his legs are tired from carrying him through the snow, which in places has drifted and is unexpectedly deep. The Marlin is heavy now, but still he runs. Runs after the sound of the deer, after flashes of the white tail, though he begins to suspect he'll never catch her, that the deer will disappear into the trees and never be found. When he reaches the stream, he follows its bank for a time but then veers back in the direction of the fence. Hears the deer moving that way, hears her without seeing her. His lungs feel bruised, on fire. He sees movement just behind a line of trees, beyond the dense foliage that tangles the woods. He lifts the rifle and fires without aiming, and then he pumps the lever and fires again, and after the third shot he moves forward through the undergrowth, ducking beneath the spiderweb of vines, and sees the bright-red blood on the snow.

And only when he steps free of the tangles does he see the maroon-colored winter coat and the boots and jeans. The man's hair is brown with gray streaks. Except for the part of his skull that appears like a raw gash, like the open pulp of smashed fruit. One of the man's arms is twisted at an angle beneath his body, the man's face pressed into the snow. To his right, still attached with a leather strap around his neck, are black binoculars. The man isn't moving or speaking. He has become part of the woods, as though he is no longer his own self but belongs to the trees and the bushes and the snow. Henry stands at a distance, watching. He waits for the man to rise from the snow, to stir. A cold wind is washing through the empty limbs of the trees. He listens to the wind, sees two squirrels chasing each other far away. He tries to imagine what he will say to his father. He tries to picture the tight anger on his father's face. And he knows he is already late for his chores. He knows his father will yell. But what will happen if he learns about this? This? He sees, before him, that acorns have dropped on the ground, sees the blood so bright against the snow. And still he watches for the man to rise, and he remembers that dream of the moon splitting into pieces. He imagines his life as like that now, coming undone, scattering. And he thinks of the thick trees and the undergrowth and the white bellies of the deer. Finally, he turns and walks toward home, moving slowly, his head down. He tells himself he will walk into the garage and sneak the rifle back into its place. He tells himself he will nod *hello* to his father, will apologize for being late, and will not speak another word. Then he will begin his chores.

The Green Bridge

In the open space where the pickup used to be, in its emptiness, there existed now mostly gravel and purple fruit droppings from the mulberry tree. Depending on the time of day, there was also shade from the open awning of the garage, a small structure housing the lawn mower, the snow blower, the wheelbarrow. The mulberry cast its shadow, too, an elongated shadow, the same type the mailbox cast on up County Route 9, though the narrow sliver from the mailbox was so small it sometimes seemed ready to disappear.

Dylan, thirteen, watched the driveway and the shadows from the windows of the bedroom he shared with his younger brother, Jack. He could see the absence of the pickup equally well from the kitchen windows. And often when he went outside, when he stood beside the mulberry, he could almost feel the pickup's presence.

Jack, on the other hand, ten that summer, focused on the crows. Always they were everywhere around the yard, black stains in the sky in the direction of the river, calling from the woods, gathering in the field across the road. They had their dark bodies to claim the landscape. One day he saw two of them feasting on a dead raccoon not far from the house, up on the asphalt by the rusting speed-limit sign. Every time a car or truck went past, the crows shuddered their veils of wings and rowed away. It was a pattern: first the crows came, then a car came, and then the crows went. It seemed to Jack, as well, that two things had occurred back-to-back that summer: his father had thrown a suitcase into the back of his truck and had driven off, and then the crows had appeared in greater numbers than before.

On Saturday—the same day Jack was witnessing the dance of the crows—Dylan went into the backyard by the clothesline and asked his mother if he could play at Wesley Hupple's house. His mother was wearing a turquoise bathing suit, lying on a yellow plastic reclining chair, and reading one of her fat paperbacks. In their father's absence, their mother seemed diminished somehow, smaller in her own space. She squinted up at Dylan out of a mist of coconut-lotion smell.

"Is Jack going?" she asked.

"I think he's watching TV," Dylan said.

"Did you ask him?"

"Wesley doesn't want him there."

"Since when?"

"Since forever, Mom. Can I go or not?"

Dylan started in the direction of Wesley's house, and after he crossed the road where the raccoon was spilling its innards, giving itself to the world, he stepped into the bean field. He kept up the pretense until he reached the tree line and the river. But instead of crossing the footbridge, he cut south and followed the muddy waters until he reached what everyone called the Green Bridge—though it wasn't green—not far from the First Baptist Church of Grace. The cemetery waited in the distance by Biddle Road, and he could see the line of railroad tracks on their raised bed of rocks, and he could see, closer in, Julie Krietemeyer in her short-shorts, her dark T-shirt, and her flip-flops. She was waiting with a blanket underneath one arm, waiting with her sunglasses darkening her eyes. She was fourteen, a year ahead of Dylan in school.

Their usual habit—and the one they stuck to on this day—was to spread the blanket on the incline at the east end of the bridge, there in the open dirt, out of sight of cars going by. From that vantage point, they could see the concrete underside of the structure—like the inside of a body, the thing you weren't supposed to see—and hear the sounds of the occasional car or truck rumbling overhead. They slapped at the mosquitoes, listened to the bored songs of birds, and watched the dirty water slipping past.

One day Dylan had caught a brown snake beneath the bridge and had banged it against a willow tree until it had stopped struggling, a loose rope. But on this day, like most, they lay back on the blanket and kissed until their mouths felt raw, until their tongues grew sticky and dry. It was slow time, stopped time, or maybe there wasn't any time at all but just the way their eyes closed and mouths joined. Later, when Julie lifted off her shirt and undid her bra, he kissed the pink and brown of her nipples, ran his calloused hands across her breasts, cupping one in his palm like an apple—only this one grew from the body of a girl. Her lips tasted of strawberry lip gloss. At one point she stuffed her hand down his jeans. He thought of a fire roaring out of the woods to overtake a neighborhood, with nothing you could do to stop it, or the sound of a train up on the high tracks, rumbling the earth, drowning out everything else. When they were done, Julie pulled her hand away, wiped her fingers with a leaf.

"Can you make it tomorrow afternoon?" she asked.

"Three o'clock?"

"Okay." Her voice was thickened but also reedy. She said, "Think about me until then."

"All right," Dylan said.

JACK HAD FOUND A stick at the side of the road, just past the bar ditch. It was a good stick, just long enough that he didn't have to venture too close to the dead raccoon. It was important to give death its space, its breathing room. He used the stick to poke the creature—it had flies with bright blue on them, flies hovering around the body, flies that flew up each time Jack poked. Once when he had gone fishing with his father, they had dragged a catfish to the bank and had left it there waiting dead—to be taken home and fileted, breaded, and fried—and it hadn't moved until Jack had touched it with his finger. Then, out of nowhere, possessed, the fish with its thick, muddy body and long whiskers had started shaking as though to free itself of the world. It was living again, if only for a moment.

It was not until his brother stepped from the field at the far side of the road, his hands in his pockets, that Jack saw him. He said, "Remember when we caught those catfish with Dad?"

"No," Dylan said.

"One flopped around after it died." Jack added, "When do you think he's coming back?"

Dylan took the stick from his brother and lifted the raccoon part way, revealing its underside. The dark stain of blood was primitive enough to demand a moment of silence from both boys. Dylan said, "How would I know?"

"I bet it's soon," Jack said.

"Why would you bet that? Why would you bet anything? You sound stupid."

Jack grabbed back the stick and threw it in the grass. It made a sound like a hiss. "You don't know anything," he said.

"Well, maybe he's not coming back," Dylan said. "That's my bet. Satisfied now? Go back to playing with your imaginary friend. Okay? That shows how smart you are."

"Shut your face," Jack said.

DYLAN THOUGHT OFTEN OVER the next few days about the smell of the loam beneath the bridge, the way the structure trembled faintly each time a car or truck went past, as though the world were about to transform to something else. And he thought about that first moment Julie would lean in his direction, how he couldn't breathe because suddenly his mouth was covered. He tried at times to picture her other places—some years they had ridden the same school bus—but on those occasions she had never seemed real, not actually herself. He imagined her waiting in front of her limestone house with her backpack, or saw her sitting with Natalie Wrigley, both giggling over nothing, but those thoughts were more like a dream, or maybe the moments beneath the bridge were the dream. All he knew for sure was that the Julie he'd seen other places—in their Sunday school class, for instance—had seemed stuck-up and even fake, while the Julie beneath the bridge was almost too real, as powerful as the pull of a planet or a star.

Thursday, when his mother was at work, he arrived at the bridge and saw that Julie was without her blanket. She began speaking at once, saying something about her parents and a cookout, but the words felt so far removed from kissing that he didn't pay them any mind. Only slowly did it occur to him that she wanted him to follow her. She started up the side of the ravine, and for the first time they crossed the bridge together, high above the secret spot where they had so often lain hidden, though from up above it didn't seem like anywhere special. He followed her into the small neighborhood beyond the bridge, the small scattering of rural houses. A fat black dog came up to greet them on the sidewalk. The dog—named Bear, Julie said—belonged to a neighbor. It wiggled excitedly, slobbered.

"Here's where I live," Julie said. The single-story pillbox-shaped house had a small garden bed of flowers, and in that bed was a little brass sign that read WELCOME, stuck into a patch of reddish mulch. It might have been anyone's house, no one's house—the sort of place you would pass by in a car without a glance—yet Julie carried on her life inside it, separate from her life beneath the bridge.

They lay together on the living-room couch, and on this occasion, for both of them, for the first time, all their clothes came off. She touched him and he touched her, though he wasn't precisely sure what he was supposed to do, or how. There was a mystery surrounding such matters, like books you read in school—you knew there was a meaning there, perhaps profound, but it was beyond your reach. She kissed him hard and breathed heavily. They were past words, past language of any sort. There was only the fever of touching, the kissing, and the slickness of their bodies.

After that they dressed, and she reached out a hand. He thought of a condemned man being led to the gallows or a firing squad. He thought of how easy it was to give yourself over. She led him down the hallway through an open door into her bedroom.

"What do you think?" she said.

There was a bed with a white and blue comforter, a dresser beside the window, an open closet door, a steamer trunk with a purple blanket atop it, some candles on top of that. There were a few posters on the walls. He tried to imagine forming an opinion, the way you might about the chances of a football team winning a game, but what he mainly thought about was that Julie slept in that room, brushed her hair there, was surely often in that space undressed. He knew he was supposed to speak, so he said, "It's nice."

She gave his hand another tug.

The next stop was her parents' room. The place smelled differently than the rest of the house—muskier, somehow, old-fashioned. She led him into the walk-in closet. There, in the narrow confines, was the strong smell of cedar chips and tightly-packed clothes. There was a light bulb on the ceiling that came on when she yanked the string. There were two rows of clothes on long bars. It was like climbing up into the attic of someone who had long ago died. Julie went up on tiptoes and pulled from the shelf a shoe box.

"Wait till you see this," she said.

The revolver she pulled free was black and small, and had a hard plastic handle with strange ridges. It was a thing that drew your eye and demanded you look nowhere else. The barrel was made of metal and had a tiny sighting nub at its tip. Dylan felt differently in its presence. She let him hold the gun in his hand, and it was heavier than he expected, as though the weight of what it could do made it physically more substantial. He touched the cylinder, which was slightly lighter in color—a strange gray-black—while the trigger was dark black again. He stared at the trigger.

"It's my Dad's," Julie said. "He lets me shoot it sometimes."

"Are there bullets?"

From the shoe box she drew out a much smaller green box with a flap on one end. There was a picture on the cover of a single upright bullet, standing at attention. She opened the flap and showed him the shiny rows inside.

"I've never shot a gun," Dylan said.

"It jumps in your hand," Julie said. She pointed to a tiny lever behind the cylinder. "That's the safety. You keep it this way so it won't go off by accident."

"Can I try?" he asked. The words filled the air between them.

She twisted her fingers into the empty belt loops on his jeans. "Don't you think you'd put a hole in the wall?"

"I mean outside."

She took a deep breath. "Just one shot."

In the woods out back, the trees made a solid canopy above them, as though protecting them from the sky, as though closing them in, keeping them imprisoned. The smell of loam was as powerful as underneath the bridge. The woods were ancient, somehow, as old as the moon at night, darker and cooler than the world of the back lawn. Dylan aimed at a squirrel about halfway up the trunk of a maple. The squirrel was innocent, he knew, had no notion what was coming. He felt the explosion in his palm. It surprised him even though he was expecting it, even though he was waiting for it. The revolver jumped like a wild creature trying to get loose. It had its own view of things, its own understanding. Dylan didn't hit the squirrel or even, it seemed, the tree. The bullet disappeared without having made any known passage through the world. After that he and Julie were running back to the house, laughing, watching for neighbors to peek their nosy selves out of back doors.

It seemed to Jack, at first, that the voices were buried in his dream. Or maybe they were inside and outside his sleep at the same time. The voices were muffled, somehow, vibrating, a wake of water rushing toward you, sweeping past, altering the world but so softly you almost couldn't be certain it was true. For a time he thought the voices were wind or maybe rain, or maybe they were leaves you walked through in the fall, your shoes kicking them up into the air. Then he woke—he had the bottom bunk, his brother the top—and knew they were actual voices coming from his mother's bedroom. He touched the wall to make certain they were real. He imagined the voices entering his palm, running slowly through his body.

He didn't know how late it was, but it was dark at the window, black in the room. He felt so groggy he wasn't entirely certain he wasn't still asleep. He touched his ear to the coolness of the plaster. One voice was his mother—the other his father. It was hard to tell if they were arguing, but, if so, it was the kind of arguing that couldn't decide if it was serious or a game. In any case, right there, just past the thin partition of the wall, was his Dad.

DYLAN WOKE IN THE morning with his first thought about the moment when the gun had tried to lunge free, about its small fury and desperation. His second thought was of Julie on the couch with nothing but her body. She had a wash of freckles running down her neck, had the knobs of her skinny elbows and knees. She was herself and nothing else, her own exact being. There were a few stray tufts of hair between her legs.

It wasn't until he was getting dressed that he glanced outside to the driveway. There was a moment, then, when the world went loose on its hinges, like a screen door ready to fall off. Once he'd seen a moon so fat and red in the night sky he'd thought the sun had fallen amid the trees, a glowing coal. He went at once to the lower bunk bed, shook Jack awake.

"What's going on?" Jack said.

"He's back."

"I know."

"How could you?" Dylan asked.

"I heard him through the wall."

"Shit," Dylan said. "Get dressed."

"He'll probably take us to IHOP," Jack said, hopping into his jeans.

Years later, in school, Dylan would learn a word that fit perfectly those first weeks at summer's end after his father returned. It was as though the word and events were connected with a kind of permanence and symmetry, as though the word was meant for that one experience and no other. The word was *bifurcated*. Half of his world remained the same—Julie beneath the green bridge, Julie at her house, Julie with her skin—but the other half was something more stark and unsettling, but no less demanding of his energies. It was something like a shadow watching from the woods, biding its time, waiting.

At first—those first days in late July, then August—his father sat on the couch with them, watching television, sat there as though this were a normal thing, something they should accept, his arm around their mother, teasing. He bought them gifts—a catcher's glove for Jack, a first-base glove for Dylan—and taught them in the backyard the technical aspects of fielding. He'd been a star in high school, everyone said, pointing it out the way you might point to a place on a map, as though everyone should know it. And to Dylan's great surprise, his father was patient with his sons when they made mistakes, only sometimes letting his eyes show a more familiar momentary flash.

"Watch the ball all the way into the glove," he said.

On Sunday afternoon he took them bowling. He might as well have told them they would be climbing aboard a spacecraft for a distant planet. Afterward they went for ice cream, the four of them crowded into the front of the pickup, jammed together until you almost couldn't breathe. The truck, then, was a kind of lair, a place where you might sleep in winter while you were hibernating. Their father let Jack drive on the back roads coming home, pretending to be ready to jump out at any moment, teasing that he knew just how to roll to safety in a bar ditch. It was a joke he kept repeating like the refrain from a song. Their father's dark hair was long in back that summer, and Dylan watched their mother twist her fingers through it, making tiny braids or mysterious designs. She wasn't looking at the hair but out the windshield at the narrow dusty road, and yet her fingers twisted and twirled, without pause, making of the hair whatever they wanted, whatever they desired. Dylan kept waiting for his father to push her hand away, to make a face liked a wrecked car at the side of the road, but instead he leaned toward her and kissed her above the ear.

There were thunderstorms that summer in the late afternoons, even after school resumed. Dylan was, for the first time ever, in high school. He was older now. You could walk down hallways and know this was your life. Each day gray clouds rolled in from the west, drifting in the Ohio sky above the fields and river and the houses, ominous and threatening, asserting their dominion. It was impossible to tell exactly when the rain might start, exactly when the thunder would growl or lash out, when lightning would dart suddenly to earth. Some days, in fact, the storms were all bluff and bluster with no actual rain. This was how Dylan thought about things with his father. It was his habit to watch his father's hands. They might be motionless in his lap or maybe still on the kitchen table, but that was never the whole story. Dylan had long ago learned to watch for that one little motion that something was waking up, the way you might study a coiled snake.

On Thursday after school he went to meet Julie again at the Green Bridge. Her body was always present now in his thoughts. He walked along the river, the sun bearing down its firm hand on the back of his neck and arms, the way grass touches ground. He looked at the sun through the trees and felt the brightness seep into his thoughts, making them dizzy.

For a time he sat beneath the bridge, listening for the occasional car going past, watching the patient passage of the muddy waters make small dustings of brightness on the surface. Always there was a world going on about its business, and always you could only watch and marvel.

After about forty-five minutes, he realized Julie wasn't going to appear, wasn't going to sit with him in the dirt and lean toward him with closed eyes. He walked back home beneath the warm sun, carrying the heat on his body the way you might carry a backpack or push a wheelbarrow loaded with stones. He walked, as well, with the thought that his father's pickup might be waiting in the gravel. First he tried to picture the truck existing there, and then he tried to picture the truck vanishing, a strange little dust devil swirling up in the place where the truck would never be again, dancing its tiny magic into the weeds.

THE BOY'S NAME, JACK knew, was Travis Corey. He smelled like something was decaying on his skin, something you might smell on a sluggish stream. If there was algae there, you might lift it out in great rancid strings, might wonder how much more there would be to keep pulling and pulling into the world. Jack knew the boy from school. He was new, having moved from Indianapolis over the summer, a place that seemed as far away as California. There was something about the boy you couldn't help seeing as an insult to every other boy who'd ever lived. Each time he spoke, it was like the words got caught in his throat and couldn't get out, or they tripped on his tongue or multiplied. Sometimes he opened his mouth to speak and nothing came out, maybe a little breath of expelled air.

Things were at their worst on the bus. In the close quarters you could smell Travis from several seats away.

"You smell like something died," Jack pointed out one afternoon.

"I d-d-d-o not," Travis said.

"You smell like someone dug you up from a grave."

Jack envisioned bones in the earth, a few flaps of flesh still clinging to the scaffolding of the skeleton. He meant to say more, but his stop was coming up. The school day was over, the afternoon making its transition to home. You weren't supposed to stand until the bus came to a complete stop, but he put his hand on the seat in front of him, ready to lift himself. A few moments later he was stepping down into the street. The door whooshed closed behind him. He saw his father sitting on the front porch, waving and lifting a beer bottle to his lips. The sight of his father was an antidote to everything else in the world. Jack ran full speed to reach him.

IT WAS AT HIS locker at school, between classes, while the hallway was a swarm—Dylan imagined two schools of fish swimming past each other in a narrow channel, in opposite directions, neither one wanting to give way—that Julie appeared before him. She reached out and handed him a small plastic bag.

"What's this?" he asked.

"For you," she said.

Inside the bag, which crinkled as he opened it, was a small wrapped box with a red bow on top. Dylan felt the obligation of holding it. And in the fluorescent lights of school, so far from the Green Bridge or even the couch at her house, Julie looked different. Her hair was almost reddish, for one thing. She had on a tan skirt he'd never seen before.

She said, "We need to talk."

"What about?"

Her gaze burrowed in, grabbing on. "We need to stop meeting," she said.

"What?"

"We're both too busy now that school's on. I'm in marching band."

He felt himself blinking. He said, "I don't understand."

"It's over, Dylan."

She turned and stepped into the crowd. Dylan was reminded now of birds taking flight, of a chaotic thrashing of wings. A few days earlier several hundred starlings had spent a half hour in the field behind their house. The birds had dropped to earth in unison, had lifted back together into the air. The students rushing past were like that.

In the box was aftershave. There wasn't a card. He turned the gift over in his hands, then threw it into the trash bin outside the restrooms. He heard it thump, then looked down to see it. It existed there without him.

WHEN JACK WOKE AGAIN in the night, woke in the deep dead of it, there were voices once more. He'd been chasing something in his dream, or maybe being chased. The voices weren't from his mother's bedroom, he didn't think, but probably from the living room, or maybe the kitchen, though they were the kind of voices that couldn't be pinned to any one place, couldn't be restricted or defined. The voices—mostly his father's— burrowed through the walls to make their way to where he lay. Jack raised himself, then stood on his bed so he could poke his brother in the top bunk.

"They're fighting," he said.

Jack followed Dylan from the bedroom, both of them in bare feet, both in pajamas, the way you might flee from a house on fire—though they headed *toward* the flames. By the time they made it to the kitchen, the voices had ceased. Everything was quiet. Their mother was leaning over the sink, and their father held a towel to her nose. There was a bright splotch of blood on the towel, as distinct as a stain on a carpet.

"Go back to bed," their father said, his arm around their mother.

"You all right, Mom?" Dylan asked.

"Did you hear what I said?"

DYLAN'S WORLD NOW WAS nothing beyond his same small obsessions, the days orbiting forever around them. At school he caught glimpses of Julie, mostly in the cafeteria at noon, and something went loose inside him, gave way, rolling in a small avalanche.

Then there was life when the truck was in the driveway or just arriving: the great gust of its engine, the squeaking of its brakes, the metallic slamming of the door. The truck was a world unto itself, its own small country. His father barreled into the house, stomping down halls or throwing open the refrigerator to grab a beer, turning up the television. His father was all exasperated sighs and grunts, all agitation and frenzy.

The only respite—if Dylan was honest with himself—was at the bridge. He walked across the field, then followed the river until he reached it. The first leaves of the season were just starting to fall, landing in the muddy water, carried off like strange boats to a destination they couldn't choose.

Sometimes he sat in the dirt where he used to sit with Julie. Her body wasn't there any longer, of course, and his body wasn't the same without her presence, but still it was like the feeling when you passed a house where you'd lived once many years ago. Often he threw stones in the river, watching the splashes causing a moment of commotion before disappearing. He lay back and closed his eyes. There was the smell of the mud, the sound of cars going past on the bridge. There was the feeling in his body that each moment stretched out and out in a straight line, threatening to grow so thin that soon it wouldn't be there at all.

One late afternoon he walked all the way to Julie's house. He saw the American flag in her front yard, watched the sprinkler arcing one way then another. Nothing had changed there— nothing knew how to change or even how to want to.

It was a little more than a week after that, on a Saturday, that he saw her. He was coming up along the river. He was carrying a stick—he'd been contemplating throwing it into the current, watching the way it might deposit itself in the moving liquid, becoming part of that new world—when he felt a sharp jab inside him. The stick fell of its own volition to the earth. She was lying on a blanket beneath the bridge. Dylan, slowly, recognized the boy she was with. Sean something. Sean Notley, maybe. A senior. On the basketball team. Dylan registered these facts the way you might check your math in a homework problem. Sean was kissing Julie with his hand up her shirt. Dylan, still walking toward the bridge—though he had slowed considerably—turned back toward home when he saw that.

It wasn't until Tuesday that he returned again to the Green Bridge, and then again on Wednesday. He couldn't stop himself, couldn't bring himself to walk anywhere else, to place one foot before the other in any new direction. Julie was never there. He saw Sean at school, strolling down the hallway by the library, living his life as though he had never been beneath the bridge at all. On Saturday Dylan walked again along the river, slowing at the exact moment when he might see if they were there. Then, after standing in the spot where Sean and Julie had lain together on the blanket—the same blanket, to be sure, against which Dylan and Julie had lain, seeing the same underside of bridge, the same slow passage of the river—he kept walking all the way to her house. He found a spot halfway down the block, partly hidden. The oak tree he stood beside, he guessed, had been watching Julie's house for as long as the neighborhood had existed, had been sitting in that spot, maybe, from before there were any houses there at all. He tried to watch the house the way the tree watched it, to feel what a tree might feel, but he couldn't. Then, without warning, the garage door opened. A few moments after that, a maroon-colored car—a Camry, Dylan believed—emerged, turning out of the driveway, heading straight down the road toward him. It seemed to know he was there, seemed to be seeking him by the tree, perhaps with a question or an accusation. He could see the mother and father in the front seat, could see Julie in back. This was the first time he'd ever seen her with her parents, but still she seemed separate from their existence. He ducked behind the trunk and felt his anger tightening in his belly like a fist. Julie was talking to her parents from the back seat, smiling, gesturing with her hands.

Years later he would look back at the moment and marvel. There are certain instants in our lives that take on an added significance, that burn a permanent place in our memories. Once the car was out of sight, he meant to head home, to walk past the bridge and follow the line of the river, but instead, out of nowhere, he found himself walking toward Julie's house, crossing the front yard, stepping past the WELCOME sign and the reddish mulch. He thought of homing pigeons on their predetermined course. When Julie had brought him there before, she had used the kitchen door, so he used it as well. It hadn't been locked then, wasn't now. He turned the knob and found himself inside. It was as simple as that, but also, in some ways, as impossible.

For a moment he stood there, stock still. There was a smell of something that had been cooking on a stove—maybe bacon grease. There was a stack of mail sprawled across the kitchen table. It was strange to look out the window, to observe the world from a vantage point where you didn't belong, like seeing people you had never seen before and never would again.

He walked down the hallway—not to Julie's room but to the parents' room. He walked into the closet and looked for the overhead light. He found the string and gave it a tug. At first he couldn't find the shoe box—there were sweaters stacked in rows, a small suitcase, a baseball cap—but then he saw it. He pulled down the shoe box and drew out the small gun, the box of bullets. The pistol was even smaller than he remembered—it fit in his palm like a secret. He ran his finger across the short passage of the barrel, ran his finger over the cylinder, ran his finger over the hard plastic of the handle. If you touched a thing like that, it was yours.

He carried the weapon to Julie's room, sat on the bed. He didn't go through her drawers or closet, didn't try to imagine her life there. Her life was separate from him now.

What went through his mind while he was sitting there was hard to say. Later—in the coming weeks and months—he would try to remember. He would picture himself waiting, would feel the turmoil of his thoughts and emotions. What he did know was that the longer he held the gun in his hands, the more he imagined pointing it at Julie's chest. He didn't want to shoot her, exactly, but the gun had its own uses and its angers, and he was subject to them. The gun knew how much it hurt sometimes to draw in a breath.

But even as he saw himself lifting the gun as Julie returned to the house, as she stepped into her room, he thought, as well, about pointing it at his father, maybe while he was lying in bed asleep. His father's hands might be twitching in a dream. His long hair would curl across the pillow. He saw himself touching the gun softly to his father's temple, drawing an X there with the barrel, the way you might draw a design in chalk on school playground cement.

After that he thought about touching the gun to his own chest, or putting the cold barrel in his mouth, feeling its metallic bite against his tongue. The first time he'd tasted Julie's tongue against his own, it had seemed to him it was a small and beautiful creature, slick in its own juices, probing. He imagined the tongue of the barrel prodding toward the back of his throat. He thought of the way a gun leaped forward in a hand.

None of that happened. For a long while he simply sat there, holding the weapon lonely in his lap, twirling it. He sat for maybe fifteen or twenty minutes—time, then, was like being in school and knowing that the period had just ended yet you hadn't heard a word, nothing of what was said about algebra or American history or a novel by John Steinbeck. The gun was in charge now, and yet it cared nothing for his feelings or resentments, nothing about who he'd been or might be in the future, if there was one. The gun cared only about the solidity of its own being, its presence in the world. Dylan stood. He didn't mean to but found himself on his feet. It was all beyond him now—the gun, his feelings about Julie and his father, the pumping of his heart in his chest. He went into the parents' bedroom and placed the gun back in the shoe box, the bullets back there, too. He put the shoe box in the closet, pulled the string and the light went out. His actions, after that, were a sequence, first one then the other. He walked down the narrow passage of the corridor, then back into the kitchen. The mail was still sprawled across the kitchen table. He went out the door and closed it behind him, walking down the street past the tree where he'd hidden while Julie and her parents had driven past. He touched the tree as he went by, but surely it could barely sense that or care, living as it did so close to the distance of the clouds. He walked to the Green Bridge, then took the steep path down to the river's edge. The river flowed green and brown, moving slowly somewhere far away. Here was the spot where the world began, then ended. He followed the river until he reached the field that led back toward his house. When he reached the road, he looked to see if his father's pickup was waiting in the driveway. Looking there was a reflex by now, built into his body. A few leaves had fallen from the mulberry tree, had lodged themselves down around the windshield wipers. Dylan took a deep breath, readying himself. He waited for maybe a beat of two or three seconds—then stepped inside the house.

The Old Worlds

I t began in August. By December it was done. All he remembered, afterward, was the freckling of light on the living-room couch where she drew him down on the occasions he went to her house. The home was on the outskirts of town, few other houses surrounding it, and she didn't seem to care where he parked, didn't care whether he walked in plain sight to the front door, didn't care that her husband would be home soon. All he remembered, afterward, was how one afternoon she told him there were ants in her kitchen sink, asked him to spray them with a bug spray, which he did. The next day, then, by coincidence, his wife informed him there were ants in the basement of their own house. He went down the cement steps to see them gathering exactly the way they had in the sink, though this time by the center drain, a strange line of them heading off to nowhere. Two years after the affair, he learned that the woman and her husband were going to have a child. And though it made no sense, he fantasized that the baby inside her had been made by him on the living-room couch with its view of farm fields out the back picture window. The child, in his fantasy, would grow up never knowing his or her true father, would be haunted by the thought. A little more than a decade after that, the woman was diagnosed with breast cancer and lost both of her breasts to surgery. That was the same winter the power lines came down in an ice storm, and everyone went for days without electricity. His wife always seemed to be sniffling that January, always coughing with a cold. Then it was summer, and often he heard crows cawing from the field behind where he lived with his wife and children. The birds had primitive voices, as though they were calling from the old worlds. And he learned after that—both he and the woman still worked in the same building—that she had died. He had been planning to visit her at the hospital, but he hadn't. And now that she was gone, he imagined that what had occurred years earlier was a secret he carried in his chest, the way the earth some nights seems to carry the moon on its shoulder. Within a few years he convinced himself he had loved the woman, that she had been the great and only love of his life. Again and again he tried to picture her face as she had drawn him down onto the couch, tried to envision the sweep of her hair, the slight parting of her lips, something. But what he mainly saw was the freckling of the light on the couch, and then, clearer still, the ants crowding in the bowl of the sink.

Dog Memories

It must be the stillness of a morning sky, the repose of grass in a field beyond a fence, or maybe the kitchen floor where my father is forever dying of a heart attack when I am five, fat doves singing outside the windows of our rental house in rural Ohio. It seems possible to remember the half-life of light on a leaf outside my childhood bedroom window in dead summer, to construct an impression from the mud of the river or the black clothes of the mourners, to dream an open maw of earth. My memories of my father are as imprecise as footprints filling with snow, though I do recall, a few months later, a bulldog coming toward me—after we were evicted from the rental home—on the porch of my grandfather's house, the creature lunging, then hovering above me. In my vision the beast snares me with his great teeth pressed against my neck, though years later my mother claims the dog was simply exuberant with friendliness and knocked me down. But if I close my eyes, I feel the animal heat of breath against my skin, the sharpness of teeth. Or maybe, it sometimes seems, memories transform to living organisms, evolving or devolving, breathing and letting go, asserting whatever volition they can. I am eleven when my mother's live-in boyfriend begins locking our German shepherd in the basement, which is a sign, we know, that he plans to beat one of us, or maybe both. The basement, as I remember it, is small and low-slung, with bare cement and a naked light bulb, cobwebs having their conversations with the hot or cold air breathing through the vents. I remember blood oozing from my mother's nose, the swollen baptism of an eye, the dustiness of memory growing more opaque yet powerful with decades, as though the past becomes a dust devil swirling its magic in August, rising from the dry earth to make itself into a living being. We are homeless, then, residing in my mother's car, the cold winter air a judgment. Once my mother is given a frozen turkey at a food pantry, and we bring it back to the Ford, uncertain how to cook it. I remember how heavy the turkey feels when I hold it in my lap, and I recall—digging deep into memory—building a fire from sticks and discarded newspapers and whatever dry wood we can find at the roadside. And then a skinny man with a white beard and a voice like a rabid dog is stopping his motorcycle by the bar ditch and stealing the turkey from us before we have found a way to place it above the flames. Blood trails its offering down my mother's forearm after the man lunges at her with a box cutter. And now, rising in my vision, is the man racing off on his motorcycle with our turkey clutched like a sleeping infant in one arm.

Confessions of a Cloud

I have fallen in love again with my husband. Probably this should surprise me more. For while some say the heart grows fonder, it's been fourteen years since his final breaths, since I last saw his unshaven face, gray and heavy with the stubble of old age. Yet if I close my eyes, I am sitting beside him once more at his hospital bed. He is a tall man, well over six feet, and skinny too, so that he seems in that bed like a peculiar, towering sapling. He is saving what few breaths his emphysema allows to criticize his nurses, his doctors, his children, and me. I don't hold this against him. The things that once seemed important have now slipped free of their moorings. My husband in this memory has deep-set eyes, and, as he has shed weight from his illness, they have receded even farther inside his skull, growing smaller and meaner-looking than ever, watching with a savage blueness from their deep caves. In those first days following his death, I would have claimed that I didn't miss him at all, hadn't loved him for most of our time together—unless you count the first year when I was too young to realize any better. But in this vision I reach out to touch his forehead while he is sleeping, the way you might feel for a fever with a child. I grip his hand and speak in a soft voice. I want him to hear me but don't want to wake him. He is beautiful in sleep, even in death. This sounds morbid, I know, but I don't mean it that way.

I am standing today at our bedroom window. It is morning, I think. I am searching for clouds. People see anything they want in the sky, so I lean against the window sill that was built by my husband and the carpenters who worked for him, and I try to see my own life on the horizon. Maybe I am a young girl again or a sixth-grade school teacher here in Decatur, or maybe the wind is blowing from the wrong direction, and the air is growing dense and sickly sweet and burning with the soybean smells from Archer Daniels Midland. This house around me is a trilevel, and from the bedroom window I spy the privacy fence in the backyard, a roof or two of neighboring houses, and those clouds I am seeking, which appear to me suddenly as familiar as weeds, with white hair like the deadheads of dandelions. And in one cloud, I decide, waits my husband with his nightly beers. He is slumped down in a lawn chair on our screened-in porch, his shirt off. Probably he smells a little from having worked hard all day. Here is a man I once resented with what seemed the greatest passion of my life, but as he begins complaining or insulting me over something I said or didn't say or did or didn't do, then taking another sip of his beer, I confess I feel once more like a schoolgirl with a first crush. I close my eyes and listen to the way his voice makes its perfect way into the universe.

"Mom, what are you doing?" I hear from behind me.

I turn. A young woman is standing here. It appears to be my daughter, but Marjorie isn't a child any longer. It comes to me, then: she, her husband, and their son, Steven, are visiting. They drove all the way from Cleveland.

"You surprised me," I say.

"We've been waiting," she says.

"For what?"

"For you to come back down. You said you were getting a sweater." My daughter adds, "We were talking."

It is funny, I suppose, how life turns on you. Jorie is still a child in my memory, and her sister, Kate, is even smaller. It is the three of us against Larry, of course. He is the bull, we agree, and we are the china shop. In my mind Jorie is nine or ten and we are staying on Mackinac Island in northern Michigan, at the Grand Hotel. We must be on vacation. It is summer, I think, because it seems we are all wearing shorts. Larry is drunk from the night before, naturally, and he is sleeping it off, so Kate, Jorie, and I rent bicycles and ride around the circumference of the island. Our legs turn in circles, as though they might go on forever. I don't believe in spirits, but on this day Lake Huron is watching over us, and it has its dreams in the same fashion that we have ours, and all of us are full to the brim with yearning.

"Can't we stay here forever?" Jorie asks when we stop on our bicycles to look out at the expanse of Maniboajo Bay. It's a name I will never forget. It slips along the tongue. The waters are such a bright blue they surely can't be real.

"I'm not sure your father will agree," I say.

"I don't mean the four of us," Jorie says. "I mean us three. On our bikes. Right here. I don't want to ride back. Ever."

But now my child has abandoned her bike and is dragging me by the arm down to the living room. She is handing me a gray sweater I don't need, insisting I put it on. It looks like that cardigan I don't like. She sits me in Larry's leather La-Z-Boy. I imagine I hear his Glenn Miller or Jimmy Dorsey on the stereo. If he's drunk enough, maybe he will ask me to dance. But I look more closely and there is someone else sitting on the couch beside Jorie. It must be her husband. He's a dermatologist, of all things. He has a great deal of dark black hair springing from his head as though it is an over-healthy fungus. And my grandson is here, too, looking impatient, like his mother. He is gazing with unhidden boredom out the window, though I don't dare to wonder what a fifteen-year-old boy might suspect he sees in a cloud.

"You told us you would think about what we were discussing," Marjorie says.

"About what?" I ask.

"Mom, we can't keep going around this same circle. You have to let us know where you stand."

"I'm tired, Jorie," I say. "I'm not used to having guests."

"Maybe we should pick this up later," the man with the black hair says. I know his name, of course, but it is like one of those birds singing in the distance. You know what it's called and you know the name will come to you eventually.

"No," my daughter says. "She's intentionally delaying. You have to let us know, Mom, about your choice. It's us or the place we looked at yesterday. And it's not a nursing home. Quit saying that. You saw what it was like. Or would you rather come live with us in Cleveland?"

"Why would I want to live in Cleveland?" I ask. "I've never been there."

"Yes you have, Mom. You like it."

There are moments, I know, when my family thinks I am so absentminded that my heart might forget to beat. I see it in their expressions. But I think you reach a certain age when you realize there are things that don't matter very much, the daily nuisances that amount to little of any lasting matter. And so you forget the date of a birthday, or you take two pills instead of one, or you neglect to hang up the phone when you are finished. When we are younger we place a great emphasis on the here and now, as though it is the only thing, but as we age we see things more clearly. Why try to separate the sky from all the birds and the clouds? And this is what I understand now about Larry. He isn't only buried in a patch of earth in Greenwood Cemetery— he is lifting a new vinyl record album from its case or pouring Shredded Wheat into a green bowl. Or maybe he is falling again from a roof at his job or has just had surgery on his leg. And surely he is here on the couch, asking me to fetch him another beer from the refrigerator. Or maybe it's some other couch that I remember, the one that belongs to Larry's father when Larry and I are first planning to get married. The furnace in the basement is humming in and out of existence, like a great beast, and Larry is trying to get me out of my clothes. He already has my blouse and bra off, but that's not enough. A woman my age is not supposed to discuss such things, but his penis, when he is fully undressed, is so much like the man: long, thin, insistent, outspoken, and a little rude. Or maybe Larry is in the clouds outside the window today, or will be the curved knife of the moon after dark, or he will be the sounds of my own breaths when I awaken in the center of a night, not certain who I am or ought to be. A love like this grows out of the ground like an immense mountain, until soon all I see is its great body and the perfect shadow it casts across the earth.

"I want to stay here," I say to my daughter.

"We've been over this," my daughter says. "You have to listen to reason."

"The dead have their reasons," I say. "That's what I think, at least. The dead don't have to follow the rules."

This shuts her up, at least for a moment, though who is to say why or how? Such things are beyond me now. There are mysteries beyond any telling.

"I don't like this sweater," I say. "I want the blue one."

THAT NIGHT I DREAM that Larry and I are swimming naked in the Sangamon River. It is dark out, but I think there's a moon above us. We are being carried away by the current, as though it is a guiding hand. We swim in the muddy waters, but then, without warning, we are making love on an old blanket along the bank, both of us smelling of river water. I feel nervous about being seen, of course, and I'm not sure we should be doing this. I think about saying so, but Larry has his own ideas. This ought to bother me, probably, but it doesn't. It seems I've grown beyond such caring. Then we are swimming once more and he is close beside me in the water, teasing me about being careful about snapping turtles. I don't think I am worried, but maybe I am. In the dream there is just the current against our bodies and the movements of our arms and legs. Then we are making love on that blanket again or maybe in our bed in the house Larry built with his own hands, which always made him proud, or maybe in the backyard where, when the house is newly built, we sneak out on dark nights to brave the mosquitoes and the chiggers. In the dream Larry can't decide if he is a young man or an old man or somewhere in between. I let him choose. Though once I think I hear him gasping for air near the end of his life. We are kissing at this point, and I feel the scratch of his beard, and there is something so plaintive in the bristles I believe I am crying. It comes on very suddenly. But in any case it's a happy sorrow, if that makes sense. I hold Larry's hand and whisper to him in a soft voice, and then he is inside me once more, all at once, and I tell him we are too old for such things, that in any case he has died, but he jokes that he has never been one for doing what he's told. I smell alcohol on his breath, and all at once I remember how sorrowful he can get sometimes, so quiet, sitting and drinking on the porch, and I run my fingers through his hair like he is a little boy, and maybe he is. It is love we feel for each other, after all, and I defy anyone to tell us it isn't.

IN THE MORNING OVER breakfast my daughter makes a point of spooning the scrambled eggs onto my plate as though I'm too hopeless to feed myself. She is very young in my memory, sitting with her sister at this table. I think Katie is in Memphis now, but in any case I see myself spooning both girls eggs onto their plates. The girls call them *mountain eggs*. But sitting across from me with my daughter and my grandson is that black-haired man who looks so familiar, the three of them lined up as though they are the firing squad and I'm waiting for the blindfold. I think I have lived this moment before, maybe many times, and I think that each time there have been clouds above my house in the Illinois sky, all of them white or gray, not quite corporeal and not quite incorporeal.

"Robert and I talked it over," my daughter says. For some reason she is no longer spooning eggs. She has always liked her orange juice, and I watch her take a sip. She says, "We have to be honest with you."

"About what?" I ask.

"You know about what," Jorie says.

I wonder if she is talking about the sweater again. "I'm not cold," I say, to reassure her.

My daughter says, "We have no choice but to take a hard line on this."

"I want to eat my eggs," I say.

"You know what Dr. Glaser said, Mom. We can't fool around with this anymore. It's getting worse. You can't look after yourself any longer. That much is clear."

I almost ask what she is talking about, but I have learned in recent months that these are trick questions, all of them, and that nothing I say will ever satisfy.

"You call them *mountain eggs*," I say.

"Mom," Jorie says. I know that scolding tone—I use it on my own children.

"I'm right here," I say. "I'm not going anywhere."

My daughter says, "I am going to stay with you for as long as it takes. We are going to put the house on the market and pack up your things. I know you don't want this, but there reaches a point where you have to face things. You will come stay with us in Cleveland. I know you don't want this, but it's how it is. Do you hear what I'm saying?"

All of them are looking at me now, as though some curtain has come up and I'm visible suddenly on center stage. "I don't know what you want me to say," I say.

"Say you understand," Jorie says. "I know you have an attachment to this house, and I'm sorry. God knows why you feel this way. I can't imagine you were ever happy here."

"Maybe I am a little cold," I say. Then I turn to the boy across from me. He has a sad face, I think, like Larry did. I say to him, "Larry built this place with his own hands. Did you know that?"

The boy is looking closely at me now. It occurs to me he has deep-set eyes. They look blue from here, but who is to say for sure? I add, "If you see a nail, he probably pounded it in. What do you think about that?"

The boy doesn't answer, probably because his mother is talking again. And then the black-haired man is talking, too, but the truth is I stopped listening long ago. I'm not certain I know how to listen any longer. Anything you hear, after all, is connected to everything else you hear, until all the voices exist together inside your head, making their own worlds and realities. So the voices yammer on, but I am envisioning Larry with his hammer and his nails, maybe on the roof and putting on new shingles, up there with the clouds over his sun-burned shoulders, up there with his hair going gray or maybe with the reddish tints because he is still so young, and I am so deeply in love with him in that instant that it's almost more than I can bear, this man who is my husband for life. I kiss him with the memory of my lips, and how can any other voice around me compete with that?

Three Crows

I don't believe the dead concern themselves with the living. It is impossible to imagine they care how I hold my hands on this steering wheel while I drive. And surely they are indifferent that I am on this flat stretch of highway, driving north toward Van Buren County and the tiny town where I grew into adulthood. The dead are partly dreaming and partly alive, my mother thinks, though she also believes that three crows in the same tree portend bad fortune, that a muddy creek bed drying, then cracking in summer means that someone will have a miscarriage. I lost my own child—a boy—in my sixth month of pregnancy, and surely there was a dry creek bed somewhere in the world, many of them, in fact, enough to wither a host of children in the womb. I am not alone in my grief, in other words. Probably I sound bitter, and I know I am, but my husband thinks that my sorrow is carrying me north from Arkadelphia—the name for this place where we are living—to visit my mother. My husband believes I am seeking comfort, that I will likely sit evenings on my mother's back porch and drink the sweet tea she learned to make as a girl in Mississippi, where she also learned that tragedies come in threes and you should spread the cut hair from your children outside your doors and windows to ward off evil spirits. It's been six weeks since Walter Michael Davis died, and in that time I have felt only the power of his absence. My mother phoned to say she hears my son in the sounds of the wind in tall grass, in the beautiful names of the birds and wild flowers she loves. My mother claims that, when my father died, he flew off with the Cooper's hawk we sometimes saw chasing birds in our backyard, that we heard calling from the woods. My mother said she could sense his presence in that call, and I envied her for that. So, what do I plan to say when I arrive? We will sit on her back porch within sight of her birdfeeders, in sight of the creek that will be dried and cracked in the August drought, and I will ask her what it is she thinks I have done to deserve this. Did I walk into the shadow of a dark bird flying overhead? Did I allow an owl to perch on our roof while my husband and I were sleeping? I will tell her how much I resent the dead for the power they hold, resent her for imagining she is speaking to my dead son, for believing he exists half in this world and half in some other, as though his ghost is still pressing toward my breast to feed.

Opuntia

I shared the house that summer with newlyweds. My wife had died, and so I wore a badge of mourning. Black after dark, then blacker. I couldn't write, couldn't eat, but still there was something beyond the moment I could feel, something I couldn't quite identify but wanted to, that seemed to come to me only in my sleep. I imagined that it was a ritual of here and not here, now and not now, something anatomical, corporeal, like the first sliver of morning light clawing out of the desert heat, wordless as stone.

My wife and I had known each other for only three years. I could see her face, though it seemed that it had become a kind of artifice, a construct growing less identifiable with each new day. She had kept a journal for her thoughts, but even when I read the words she wasn't there, had somehow fled from her own voice. And always there were the prickly pears outside the window of the bedroom we had shared, prickly pears with their cladodes and hair-like spines sprawling beside the fence. And maybe there was a certain pattern of remembering, which isn't remembering at all but naming, this dream that makes its slow passage through the body. This is the way the earth feels when you are dizzy on *colonche*. Imagine the apprentice moon adrift in the dark sand of sky, the forgotten self absolving the years and their responsibilities. Often my wife came to me when I was drunk. I could see her then, but still there was so little we could share.

And often at night I found myself watching the newlyweds—
my housemates, my colleagues, my friends—carrying a blanket
out to where the scorpions hid. I watched through a single
crack in the drawn blinds. It was embarrassing, to be sure, but
I couldn't stop. Though who is to say what it was I hoped for or
wanted from my efforts? As a boy I had eaten candy made of
cactus figs, had imagined loneliness as the discarded skin of a
diamondback. Loneliness, now, was the sight of the lovers in
the desert, their movements. The newlyweds, after all, had their
bodies for abandoning. And the moon had its broken wheel. All
night I imagined heat rising from the entrails of the earth. I
imagined my wife returned to me and removing the glochids
from the red and purple fruit of the *opuntia*. I imagined making
candy with her from that fruit, giving it to the children in the
neighborhood. I pictured them running around us, swirling
past our legs.

And come morning I walked often into the desert near where
the lovers had spread their blanket. There was nothing there but
sand, nothing but stone. My wife had written sometimes about
the *Yucca brevifolia*, though none were there that I could find. She
had written of her own life, of her illness, neither of which any
longer existed. And as for me, I believed that the years to come
would wander: bone-white clouds skirting the moon. I believed
there was a caravan of hours, not the mud that made us but the
long trek of desert rock, this artifice of movement—ravens from
childhood, dark as decay. *I came to you like a held breath.*

And always that summer I felt the desire both to forget
my wife and to remember her. Particularly in the mornings
when first light brushed across one half of the saguaro while
the other half waited in darkness. Newness, I imagined, was
learning to see what wasn't there. And still the earth remained
ancient beyond all knowing, the wild cloud-ladders piercing
the dream world. Then one late afternoon I saw in the distance
the upright obelisk of a raven, a black figure that earlier had
floated above the exact spot where the newlyweds had made
from their nights a child I would soon see swelling the wife's

belly. I remember watching the raven watching me. And then I plucked an *opuntia* flower that had died, rolled it in my fingers, waiting for the bird to fly away. And when it did, I walked back to the house and went inside.

Baobab

He can't be certain how much he actually remembers and how much he has been told by his mother. The stories and his memories are the vine and the tree so intertwined he can't distinguish one from the next. He does know he was very young in that time before they left for the United States. His father showed him how to hide beneath the baobab tree behind their house. It was a great tree, as old as the moon—or so his father teased—with spirits waiting in the fruit from which they sometimes made a porridge. There was an indentation in the earth into which the boy and his sisters lay down, pulling across themselves what must have been leaves or twigs, though mostly he remembers being among the heavy earth smells and gazing up at the high branches of the tree, which seemed far away and, so, as beautiful as stars. Sometimes it was the soldiers going by, sometimes the rebels, though it was hard for the boy to see one as any different than the other. And it was beneath that tree that the boy's sisters lost their lives, though the boy did not witness that himself. It has been the one event that both his father and mother have refused to discuss in any detail for all these years. The three of them live now in Pittsburgh, Pennsylvania, less than two miles from the Ohio River, though the boy is not a boy any longer and resides with his wife—American born, with distant ancestors from, of all places, Norway—and their two young children, one boy, one girl. He works as an anesthesiologist at Allegheny General, and he does not have a hiding place in his own backyard, no spot for his son and his daughter to seclude themselves should the soldiers or rebels drive by with their Kalashnikovs. There is a swing set with a slide, a badminton net they leave up in the summers, and little nozzles that peek up from the earth in dry weather to dampen the grass. He does worry, of course, about what the future will bring when his children come into contact with typical city woes—thugs and gangs, drugs and unprotected sex—but for now his children are as innocent as his memories of making bread from the baobab fruit with his mother and his sisters, making sweet and sour candy from the pulp. So it comes as a shock when his wife awakens him one late August night to say she thinks she hears someone in the house. He rises at once. Tells his wife to hide in the bathtub. Crosses the hallway to the rooms of his children. Hides them at the back of their closets, covers them with loose clothes. *Stay quiet,* he says, *quiet.* Then grabs the baseball bat he keeps in the bathroom closet for such occasions, crosses down the narrow hallway into the main part of the house. Over the years he has come to believe that his sisters must have been raped before they were killed, even though they were only children—and that is the horror his parents can't bring themselves to share—and he tries, now, for a reason he isn't certain he knows, to call up the faces of his sisters. But all he remembers are the faces from the photographs he keeps atop his office desk at the back of the house. He is enraged at the thought. He has nothing left of his poor sisters, nothing he can truly call his own. And now these intruders are after his own wife, his children. He knows it is foolish, knows he should be hiding with his family, knows he should be phoning the police, but he storms into the living room with his bat raised in a striking pose. And he sees the moving beam of a flashlight. And he flips on the switch of the overhead light. And there they are. Two of them. Trying to remove his flat-screen TV from the wall. And so he goes after them. He can't say whether they have a weapon or are unarmed. He can't say anything about them except that they are here, that it is an affront, that it cannot be tolerated. They are fleeing by then, but he goes after them, and the bat finds the back of one of the thieves, knocks him against the couch. There is a satisfying grunt of air expelled from the blow, the pain of the affliction—but then something terrible happens. The intruder puts up his hands to protect his face and body, and it is clear now in the light that he is just a boy—maybe sixteen, at most—and it is clear that he is terrified by this monster before him with the bat, as terrified as his sisters must have been so many years ago. So on the one hand he wants desperately to bring down the bat, to crush the face of the child by the couch, but on the other hand he wants to stroke the boy's cheek, to tell him it will be okay, he is safe now, he has nothing to fear. In the end the man sits quietly with the boy on the couch while they are waiting for the police to arrive, both of them with their hands in their laps, neither of them speaking or looking at the other.

Jamaican Snow

I t was the story they always told at parties and weddings. But on this occasion in September, Ainsley and her husband, Robert, shared it with his childhood friend, Mark, and Mark's new wife, Melissa, at a Thai restaurant on State Street in Chicago.

They ordered drinks: Thai iced tea for her, Singha beer for the rest. Melissa was unexpectedly tall—she'd played basketball once upon a time at Indiana University—and asked, almost at once, the standard question of how the two of them had met. Robert, instead, launched into the more interesting honeymoon story, setting the romantic scene of the tropical Jamaican beach, the generous jungle mountains, and the hotel room balcony that overlooked Ocho Rios Bay.

Ainsley's role for the moment was to lean against her husband's arm, pretending to swoon a little, and then—they had worked it out over the past few years into a little choreography of narrative—to jump in with the punch line. Summoning what she hoped was a slightly wistful expression, she announced that it had been the perfect romantic getaway until they were driven up into the mountains and robbed at knife point on the banks of the White River.

The questions arrived quickly after that. Since Mark was Robert's friend, Ainsley let her husband take the lead. He launched into the full narrative, starting on the morning when rain had derailed their plans to take the hotel van to Dunn's River Falls. From her vantage point by the restaurant window,

Ainsley could see the pedestrians blurring past, a great tumble of frenetic heads bobbing by like flotsam as her husband described how they took a taxi up into the mountains. The drinks arrived just as he was reaching the story's turning point, that moment when they had first begun to realize something was awry.

"Robert figured it out before I did," Ainsley said. "I was focusing on the scenery and narrow roads. People living out of shacks and vans."

"Don't forget the dogs," Robert said.

"You could see the ribs trying to poke out of their skin," Ainsley said.

Robert launched quickly into the meat of the story, but for reasons she was having difficulty articulating, Ainsley was feeling a little miffed. The more recent conversational staple she'd been expecting—instead of the Jamaican story—had been bypassed and, apparently, abandoned. Earlier when she'd asked for tea—no caffeine—she'd glanced at Robert, waiting for him to ask, as he always did, if anyone could guess why his wife was avoiding alcohol. But somehow the opening had withered on the vine. Robert had begun talking, instead, about the laminate wood flooring they were considering for their dining room.

But it wasn't until Ainsley and her husband were on their way home in her husband's Miata that she appreciated the precise degree of her annoyance. She'd been looking forward to the evening, had been enjoying herself, and yet, practically the entire time—all through dinner and then, afterward, at a small piano bar on Michigan Avenue—the conversational trajectory had rarely varied from the twin topics of house renovations and places to vacation. Robert had made a passionate case that, despite their one bad experience, Jamaica was a lovely locale, no more dangerous than many sections of Chicago, perhaps less so. There was the friendliness of the people—despite the crushing poverty and hawkers on the streets straining to sell you anything and everything, including illegal marijuana. They'd all laughed over his rendition of the handful of words he'd learned of Jamaican patois, most moderately obscene.

So why the resentment? From the passenger side, Ainsley watched the headlights zooming toward them, then retreating, watched, in the side mirror, the receding lights of the city, which reminded her, at this time of night, of an otherworldly dreamscape, post-apocalyptic.

Robert said, "I never would have guessed Melissa would be Mark's type. What do you think?"

Ainsley, in fact, agreed, but her husband appeared so pleased with his remark, so clearly eager to launch into some analysis or another—on the walk to the piano bar he and Mark had gone on endlessly about how often they'd gotten their friends, often girls, utterly hammered back in high school, usually on bourbon from the bars of their respective fathers—that she felt compelled to deny him.

"Was there a reason you didn't mention I'm pregnant?" she asked.

Robert shot her a look. "That didn't come up?"

"No."

"I thought I heard you and Melissa talking about it."

"No," she said, adding, "You probably thought it didn't fit with your stories about getting high-school girls drunk in basements so you could take advantage of them."

His eyes narrowed. "What's going on, Ain? We didn't take advantage of anybody. Mostly we just passed out or got sick. Where is this coming from?"

"It seems to me you might bring up being a father-to-be before going on about different kinds of floor tiling." She added, "And why did you say that thing about the dog?"

"What thing?"

"You claimed the driver ran over one while we were heading up the mountain. That didn't happen."

"What are you talking about?"

"Did you think you needed to embellish the story? Do you really think it needs it?"

Her husband unglued his eyes long enough from the unspooling road that she could tell he was deciding whether to broach a certain topic, and in that instant—in that one infuriating instant—she knew exactly what it was.

"Don't you dare tell me it's my hormones acting up," she said. "Yes, I cry over stupid TV commercials, but that doesn't mean you weren't being an asshole tonight."

"Because I exaggerated a story? Are you serious?"

"He never hit a dog, Robert."

"Are you sure, Ainsley? I think I remember he did."

"It didn't happen. We both remember all of it. Every bit. We saw a lot of dogs, but he never hit a one. You know that."

And with that—and with enough dramatic flair she almost didn't recognize herself—she reached down to flip on the radio.

IN AINSLEY'S MIND OVER the next few days, in stray thoughts that arrived in empty moments—driving to and from work, unloading the dishwasher, folding laundry—she returned again and again to the events of their honeymoon in Jamaica. This was not unusual, in fairness. Her thoughts were always circling back—for almost three years now—to that uncomfortable geography. To be precise, it wasn't the honeymoon itself on which she focused but just that one day, though even with that there was the portion she was fine with and the portion she wasn't. The part she liked, if that was the right word, began always with she and her new husband awakening to the sounds of tropical rain.

The plan for the day had been to take the hotel van to Dunn's River Falls, but when they stood from bed and went out on their tiny balcony, dressed in matching terry-cloth bathrobes provided by the hotel, leaning against each other with unmitigated affection, they watched storm clouds drifting everywhere. The gray-black formations seemed to be trying to sever the lush jungle mountaintops to their right, and the ocean directly before them was awash in slanted assaults of rain. The entire world was trying to hide its secret face in a veil. Ainsley and Robert dressed, in any case, in the bathing suits, cover-ups, and water shoes suggested in their guide book, then went down to breakfast. The concierge assured them they would be getting utterly soaked as they climbed the rocks to the fall's summit. But when the time came to make the final decision about stepping aboard the van, they selected to put off the trip for the next day, when the forecast was infinitely more promising.

As always when Ainsley turned her thoughts back to that moment, she concentrated on that decision to postpone, how easy it would have been to make the opposite selection, to give herself, even now, a little retrospective nudge the other way, as though that were possible. How close, indeed, they had come to choosing the van and thus altering for the better their own personal histories.

Instead they unpacked the umbrella from the brown suitcase and left the hotel huddled contentedly beneath it, arm in arm. They were newlyweds, after all, and their appreciation for the other had never been more openly present in the air. They walked up from the beach toward town. On their provided map were directions to Taj Mahal mall, Island Plaza, and the Craft Park. It seemed a perfect day for browsing—however short the budget might be—and, despite the rain, there was the unambiguous pleasure of a temperature hovering above 80 in mid-December, and of walking together with exposed arms and legs. They joked as they passed another sprawling coconut tree how it was beginning to look a lot like Christmas.

There were many moments that morning that might have made a crucial difference, if only they had realized. First they became lost in searching for the Island Plaza and ended up, instead, at the Taj Mahal mall. Then they spent an inordinate amount of time picking out postcards and T-shirts for family and friends, all of which might have gone more quickly had a strap on Ainsley's sandal not snapped. They bought a new pair from a friendly clerk in an open-air shop, a clerk who kept lowering the price even though they made no effort to bargain.

Afterward, they noticed something remarkable: the storm clouds that minutes earlier had dominated the sky in all directions, claiming the whole of the island as an empire, had vanished. The Caribbean sun had ensconced itself above and was making its steady ascent. Ainsley recalled standing with her husband in that perfect light, both of them enjoying themselves, squinting, and trying to decide whether to keep shopping or to head out to Dunn's River Falls after all. They were, at that stage of the marriage, still in that hyper-considerate phase where neither wanted to stake out a strong position, at least not before uncovering the secret preference of the other. Ainsley loved her husband—it literally hurt sometimes, the feelings so visceral— while still recognizing a certain flaw or two, including that he was more than capable, with small matters, of being remarkably indecisive. In larger matters—at work, primarily—her husband prided himself on making firm and instantaneous decisions, trusting his instincts, so to speak, taking charge, but on the island they both hedged and delayed, making desultory efforts to list the pros and cons as a way of gauging the preferred stance of the other.

The truth was—and this is the part Ainsley couldn't help revisiting endlessly—she herself thought it made more sense to put off the trip until the next day, to get an early start and have the convenience of the hotel van. But here was a complication: she suspected her husband felt the opposite. Shopping, for him, was more ordeal than pleasure. And she supposed that if they went climbing up the falls that day it would be to his taste, the kind of adventure he enjoyed. Shopping could always be put off.

She made up her mind. "It's so beautiful out, Robert," she said, "let's go." And that, of course—not to put too fine a point on it—set everything in motion.

And because twice during their leisurely walk from the hotel to the shopping center, taxis had slowed near the sidewalk and a driver had called out to ask if they were looking for a fare, it seemed a simple enough matter to get to Dunn's River Falls. Only later would they read in their guide that they should select only JUTA cabs with license plates displaying PP or PPV. For now, though, it seemed to them that finding a way to the falls should be as straightforward as merely walking out toward a reasonably busy street.

It was. When the cab stopped at the curb and the driver leapt out to open the back door to his sedan—they agreed almost at once on a price—traffic was whooshing past in a kaleidoscope of twisting lines, colorful as pinwheels. And that was where Ainsley liked to leave matters in her thoughts. Here was the final instant, in truth, when things might have taken a different course. What if they'd wandered out to the road a few minutes earlier or a few minutes later? What if the driver hadn't spotted them gesturing at the curb? It wasn't that Ainsley couldn't remember what happened after that . . . it was that there were some memories without any profit. She preferred the summarized and sanitized version of events they reserved for social situations with friends.

NOT UNTIL THE FIFTH full day of the tiff with Robert—beginning on the drive back from the city—did Ainsley begin to wonder, grudgingly, if perhaps a wash of estrogen, progesterone, hCG, and hPL were playing some small and unwelcome role after all. It was late in the morning and she was looking out her office window. She had a view, unimpeded, of College Avenue and scores of Wheaton students milling to and from class, many appearing almost achingly youthful and expectant. Usually she found the sight invigorating, inspiring—college, in many ways, had been, for her, a favorite time of life, open to so many wild possibilities she had joked with friends that she had kept changing majors to extend it. Most days, now, she sat at her desk and thought how grateful she was to have a job that still kept her connected to that heady life. She thoroughly enjoyed her work in admissions, even if it wasn't the kind of high-powered or prestigious position her husband claimed as an attorney in the city. They had both found what they wanted, thank goodness, and that was what counted. But the truth was she hadn't enjoyed much of anything over the past few days. For reasons she couldn't say, and for reasons that made no earthly sense, she had grown increasingly furious.

It was completely unfair, she knew. Could it really be because he'd overlooked mentioning the pregnancy? Why should she care? His saying it or not didn't change the fact. A child was growing inside her—a little alien or hopeful bundle, depending on her mood—and no amount of talk changed the truth of how pleased she was. What actually bothered her, she decided, what filled her like one of those hot air balloons ready to lift from the earth and not come back, was the stupid story about the struck dog. Robert claimed he saw the driver swerve to hit it. He said he'd felt the tires bumping over the creature, had heard it yelp. And what annoyed her so utterly, it seemed, wasn't even that he'd felt the need to exaggerate, but that he'd deviated at all from the standard and predictable route of their social story. That was it, she knew, as crazy as it sounded. They'd been telling the same exact sequence of events, in the same exact way, for three years. Now her husband had thrown in, for no earthly reason, a murdered dog.

And what was the big deal? About that Ainsley still had no clue. She stood from her desk and walked to the window. A young man and woman were playing Frisbee in the grass, the girl's hair sailing its dark wing behind her as she ran. It was easy to imagine the couple walking back later to a dorm room and falling into each other's arms. Ainsley, watching the Frisbee spinning in air, tried to summon her own days on college lawns, her own days of falling into Robert's dorm room bed; but, despite herself, and despite trying to will a more appropriate response, what she mainly felt was a seething heat of resentment.

"Aren't you ever going to let this go?" Robert asked that evening.

They were watching, on demand, their latest addiction—*Shameless*—based on a British version of the same show, which, by chance, they'd seen a single episode of while visiting London fourteen months earlier . . . the only other real vacation of their marriage.

"I didn't say anything," Ainsley said, but she knew, for all that, what he meant.

"That's the point, isn't it?" he said. "You sit here like I don't exist."

"I know you exist, Robert," she said, her words appearing in air without her intending to say them, "because I can't hear what Fiona is saying."

Lifting the remote, he pressed "pause," so that Fiona froze with a bewildered expression. Robert said, "Let's have this out once and for all, okay? So I forgot to tell Mark and Melissa you were pregnant. Do you want me to call Mark on the phone and make the announcement?"

"That's not it, Robert."

"Then what?"

That, of course, was the mystery.

He added, "How many times are we going to go over this same ground? I'm sorry I didn't mention it. You could have mentioned it, of course, but apparently I'm not supposed to point that out. Apparently it's my sole obligation to bring it up or else it proves I'll make a miserable father."

"I never said that."

"Please, Ain, let's get past this. I don't know why it's such a big deal."

Ainsley, watching his fingers as he spoke, saw his thumb begin to edge slightly toward the "play" button on the remote. She saw him hesitate, considering, and it was that hesitation that put her over the edge, even though she didn't want to fall past it, even though she felt *sorry* for her husband and knew she was utterly in the wrong.

"Go ahead and watch your fucking show," she said, rising and storming toward the bedroom.

Her dreams—nightmares, really—had been in many ways the worst part after the traumatic events in Jamaica, persisting for months. Dreams, Ainsley knew—if Freud was correct—were supposed to be wish-fulfillments, but not these, not by any stretch. In some, the dark face of the driver swam up before her as though out of a muddy lake or a dark tangle of leaves, and that was enough to catapult her free of sleep. She felt guilty, of course, that the man's dark skin played a central role. He loomed before her with the black continent of his skin, far darker than was probably the case in life, and the racist implications troubled her almost as much as the feeling of his hand when he reached out for her vulnerable shoulder or to grab her by the hair, two things that hadn't actually occurred in life. She wanted the lights on, then, of course. Lots of lights. And preferably a radio or television going. And she wanted not to sleep at all, not if she could help it.

Robert, somehow, seemed less fazed, though she suspected that was partly for show, which she well understood. They didn't talk much about what had happened, and when they did it was to reassure each other how lucky they had been, how things might have been far worse. But Ainsley couldn't stop herself—not in those first weeks—from repeatedly calling up memories of the day. She hadn't yet learned to box them away, to bundle them in a closet or drawer. They had free rein and did what they wanted.

And even when she was awake, the man's face would suddenly appear before her. Often he was smiling—which had actually been the case. He was a tall man, with wide shoulders, clearly athletic, most likely in his late 20s, wearing a red T-shirt with a design neither she nor her husband could recall afterward. At one point, Robert said it might have included a song title by Bob Marley, which she didn't think was correct . . . that would have been memorable for her as well. He had on gray shorts and sunglasses, not covering his eyes but looped around his neck with what appeared to be shoe-lace string. But when, later, they provided the Jamaican constables with these details, the officers didn't seem to find any worth recording. The man had called himself Jimarcus, they had explained, but the constables didn't seem overly impressed by that either.

And while the man had been driving them ever higher into the mountains—whatever his name truly was, since surely he already knew what he was planning—he kept turning sideways and regaling them with stories about the Arawak natives, the ancient slave trade, and various landscapes they were passing. He was amused to point out the razor wire atop the walls surrounding the gated communities they passed before heading up the steep road. The higher you went, apparently, the less money you had. The extremes didn't sound that far removed from Chicago, but the driver spoke about such iniquities with enough high humor there seemed nothing ominous in it. Indeed, the only time his spirits seem to sink was when he told the story of an old blind woman who'd been run over two days earlier by a rich man not far from the Lady of Fatima Roman Catholic Church. And the rich man, our driver said, hadn't bothered to stop or to even drag the dying woman from the street.

By that time, Ainsley was mostly noticing how narrow and treacherous the mountain road had become. Their driver didn't seem to think it was necessary to put much effort into watching where he was headed—he preferred to twist about to face them—though he did honk his horn every time he approached another sudden jog in the road. "We can't both fit," he said, shrugging. Later he made a lame joke about the many potholes as a Jamaican form of massage, though he did promise to try to maneuver around most of them.

The worst part for Ainsley, in retrospect, was how thoroughly she *liked* Jimarcus at that point. His philosophy seemed not unlike the island ethos they kept hearing in a song played at the hotel: "Don't Worry, Be Happy." What's more, the local accent was endearing. Jimarcus asked them a few questions about where they were from in Chicago, and when they mentioned they were newlyweds, he pulled the sedan for a moment to the side of the road. Even after rain, the dust rose otherworldly into the air.

"Did you have curried goat at the reception?" he asked, winking. "And what about rum cake? It couldn't have been a real wedding without rum cake."

Later Robert would claim he was already feeling suspicious, not because of anything having to do with Jimarcus but because of their ever-increasing elevation. Robert had read in the guide book that the tour up the falls began at beach level, so he couldn't for the life of him understand why they were forever heading up. Ainsley, meanwhile, was more distracted by the occasional great chasms off to the side, with no railings. Jimarcus slowed his vehicle as he went around them, leaning on his horn at every turn, but she couldn't help envisioning tumbling off the side to lie dead in a jungle gully.

From Ainsley's point of view—and this was the worst part, in some ways—her first moment of suspicion came only when her husband finally spoke his thoughts aloud.

"We're headed to Dunn's River Falls, right?" he asked. "We want to start at the bottom and climb up. Are you taking us to the top?"

"Almost there," Jimarcus said.

"At the top or the bottom?"

"Almost there."

For a long while there had been old cars, trucks, loitering people, and ramshackle houses—some with broken out windows and missing doors—and the ever-present stray dogs, most cadaverous and slinking. But now there was simply the density of jungle, the sounds of birds, and the isolation of a foreign land.

Jimarcus pulled suddenly to the side of the road, bumping down a narrow rut of tire tracks, then brought the vehicle to a stop.

"Here we are," he said.

Still—still—Ainsley believed there must be a mistake. She could see, to her left, the twisting line of a river with water so pure and clear she could follow the contours of the rocks along the bottom. Strange Jamaican trees draped themselves over the water's passage and enclosed it almost entirely in dim shade. The current moved its slow dream.

"Do we walk to the falls from here?" Ainsley asked.

"No," Jimarcus said.

And this was the part—probably less than three or four minutes total, the tiniest sliver of an hour within the tiniest sliver of a year within the tiniest sliver of a life—she dreaded most remembering. Out of nowhere a knife appeared in the driver's left hand—that was another thing they had emphasized to the constables . . . he was left-handed. It wasn't much of a knife—a steak knife, surely, the sort they might offer you at a cheap steak house—with a narrow wooden handle.

"Everything valuable," the driver said. "Money, credit cards, cell phones, jewelry, watches. Be quick."

Now—even *now*—Ainsley waited for the grin, that widening smile Jimarcus seemed to pull from his body like a bird taking flight. They would all laugh, surely, and then he would guide them down the path to where they were headed.

"Are you serious?" Robert asked.

Their driver simply nodded.

Even thinking about it now, even remembering, Ainsley felt her chest tighten, her stomach fumble into knots, as though she were somehow transforming to stone . . . if stone were capable of breaking into a damp blush of sweat soaking through a blouse. "What's happening?" she heard herself asking.

"Throw it all on the front seat there," the man said, pointing. "Don't leave anything back. Wedding rings, too." He waved the knife—his wand. Some little spell was being cast. To her he added, "The purse. All of it. Don't empty it . . . toss it."

They did as instructed. Of course they did. Certainly, in one sense, an entire lifetime had passed since they'd pulled off the road. The engine was still running, the car trembling. She was trembling, too. As far as she knew, the whole world was trembling.

"Get out," the man said, pointing.

"Don't hurt us," Ainsley said. The words arrived of their own volition. They made no sense, of course. Either he would hurt them or he wouldn't. It was no different than rain falling, rain that came out of the sky, and all you could do was watch.

But before they could climb out, something happened that she and Robert never discussed after the fact, not once. She heard the words sometimes whispered in a dream.

"He's not much, is he?" the man said, inclining the tip of the knife in Robert's direction. "He sits there."

No one else spoke. There wasn't a breath of air inside the car.

The man said, "Maybe we should have him get out and you stay." He was grinning now, that flash of unexpected wings, but they seemed darker now, like crows, despite the white teeth. "I'll show you what it's like. He doesn't know. He's nothing. Someone beautiful as you . . . I'll show you a thing."

And then they were out of the car—she could never remember, actually, climbing out. But she did remember standing at last in open air, the sound of the moving river beyond her. Remembered the wind winding out of the mountain and jarring them back into the world.

And the car sped off. Gone. Disappeared around the bend, back the way it had come.

And whenever Ainsley looked back, the rest of that morning was a blur, unimportant, and had seemed so even at the time, though still an ordeal. They wandered as best they could back to the main road. Not sure whether to wave down a passing car or truck. Not sure who to trust—if anyone. Not sure if they should knock on a door of some hardscrabble shack they passed.

Then a pickup stopped, driven by a young mother and her infant child. No infant seat . . . just a mother's lap to sit in. She drove them all the way back down to town, and they promised to leave gas money for her later at the front desk of their hotel, which they did. She dropped them at the police station though advised against it, and the constables in their ridiculous bright uniforms told them the man probably hadn't been serious anyway. No actual danger. All ended up fine. Then they walked back to the hotel—staggered really—and entered the front lobby to see fake snowflakes falling from the ceiling, a great swarm of them tumbling down. Christmas music blaring from the piano. "Don't eat them," the children were warned about the falling flakes, apparently made of soap shavings.

IT WAS ANOTHER FULL week—regardless how much they both at this point clearly longed for the arguments to end—before, on Sunday afternoon, Ainsley and Robert went out together to the supermarket, both agreeing grudgingly to the joint excursion. Ainsley pushed the cart and her husband went ahead to a different aisle. She was searching for bananas—organic—but couldn't find any that weren't green. Robert came back into view, carrying Heineken, hot salsa. He liked it hotter than she did, though in any case her appetite was unpredictable these days, so anything was possible.

"You know this has to stop," he said.

She couldn't help flaring at the remark—truly, she couldn't— but she forced down a deep breath, nodding.

"I know that," she said. "I don't want to fight either."

"I'm sorry for whatever it was I did."

"I know, Robert."

"This is a hard time for you, Ain. I can't imagine what you must be going through since we found out you are pregnant. But I want things back like they were."

"I do, too."

"So, we're okay?" he asked.

She set down the green bananas in the cart. She wanted to explain how sorry she was, how she didn't really know why she'd been acting this way, but that wasn't what came out.

"Don't take this the wrong way," she said, "but I want to ask a favor." She hesitated a beat then added, "Please stop telling the Jamaican story. I want us to keep it to ourselves."

She could see him starting to respond—surely he was going to ask why, what reason she might have—but then his mouth fell closed.

After a moment, it opened again, more carefully. "Okay," he said.

"I mean not ever, Robert. Really. It's over and done. There's no point dredging things up."

"If that's what it takes," he said.

"It does."

"No problem, then, Ain. I didn't know it upset you so much. Really. It's no big deal."

"Don't forget, Robert. I mean it. Don't start drinking some night and forget."

"You have my word."

So that was that. She looped an arm through his and leaned for an extended moment against him, right there beside the produce. Though a little nagging thought did follow her later down the aisles—like the one stubborn wheel of the cart that kept turning in aimless circles rather than making up its mind—that she wished he'd put up a little more of a fight.

Crow

A t school, the playground fence made a pattern of light against the ground. It was triangular light. Chad bent down and touched the shape with his fingers. The asphalt had cracks in it out of which grass grew, out of which shapes grew.

Around him, voices lifted like waves in a distant sea. Around him, boys and girls rushed everywhere, but not too close.

Sometimes whole days passed like a whisper.

On the bus home he felt the railroad tracks jiggling beneath him. Then, past the reservoir, the doors whooshed open. He climbed down. Dust rose into the air as though ghosts were returning to the world. There wasn't another house in sight. Just yellow paint above the limestone.

"There's a snack on the table," his mother said.

Past the backyard was an open field and a thin finger of creek. Chad walked there before supper, searching. He found a small green snake and chased it through the undergrowth until it disappeared. He found a butterfly, wild and erratic in air. The butterfly couldn't decide where it was headed.

He heard his mother calling. These days it was just the two of them. His father's clothes were still in the closet, the boots still in the garage, but his mother made the absence sound like snow in winter that covers the earth and will be there forever, as though that white was as permanent as stone.

After supper his mother had to drive over to her sister's. She told him not to leave the house. In the garage, high up, he found his father's rifle. He'd learned to bring a chair out from the kitchen.

His father, back when there was snow on the ground, had taught him to work the bolt. The bullets were in a box that opened with a cardboard flap. He gripped one bullet between his thumb and forefinger, the way he'd been taught. He fed it into the opening, pointed side first.

There were crows in the field. Black wings. The color of dirt. His father had called them dirt birds. Beautiful dirt birds. Chad felt the tall grass brushing his body. Saw insects rising like spirits from the swales.

Night was gathering its dark hallway in the trees, but the light, here, was trapped. He pointed the rifle the way he'd been taught. He squeezed the trigger the way he'd been taught.

The explosion was as loud as horse hooves coming toward you in a dream.

At first, for two days, he kept the bird hidden back in the closet. It had black eyes. Black beak. You could touch the black feathers with your fingers.

Sometimes he brought it into bed with him. The bird had a quiet voice. In the field it had called out to the clouds, but now it held itself as still as the silence between heartbeats.

Crow, he called it in his thoughts. And he said, aloud, "Crow."

He plucked one feather and brought it with him to school. He pulled it out while he was sitting at his desk. He ran his fingers across it in the playground. You could stroke the feather like petting a cat.

It rained that afternoon. He climbed from the bus and found worms crawling on the driveway. He lifted one and it wriggled in his fingers. When his mother wasn't watching, he brought the worm to his room and touched it to the crow's beak.

"What stinks in here?" his mother asked when she was tucking him in that night.

He said, *Nothing*.

She said, "Something stinks in here."

He said, *Silence*.

The next day he carried Crow out the back door to his father's toolshed. There was a black tarp. He hid the bird beneath it.

He dreamed that night that the bird had been nailed to a tree and was trying to escape. The wings thrashed. The bird made a sound like an angry wasp.

On Saturday he carried the creature into the field. The thin trickle of creek was a living brown. He held the bird's beak to the water.

Drink, he thought.

Later he held Crow in his palms, then threw the bird up into the air.

Fly, he thought.

He brought Crow back into the house, down into the basement. His mother's washing machine and dryer were a restless thrum. He sat on the cement floor with Crow in his lap.

He closed his eyes and pictured the return of winter. Saw snow falling from the sky, making everything the same. Imagined snow covering Crow until even his wings were white. Imagined Crow lifting into air while white flakes battered his body.

Doug Ramspeck teaches at the Ohio State University at Lima. His prizes include the John Ciardi Prize for Poetry, selected by Leslie Adrienne Miller, the Barrow Street Prize, selected by Mary Ruefle, and the Michael Waters Prize from Southern Indiana Review Press. A graduate of Kenyon College and the University of California at Irvine, he lives in Lima with his wife, Beth Sutton-Ramspeck. They have a daughter, Lee, who lives in North Carolina. *The Owl That Carries Us Away* is his first fiction book. He is the author of five books of poetry.

Winners of the G. S. Sharat Chandra Prize for Short Fiction

A Bed of Nails by Ron Tanner, selected by Janet Burroway

I'll Never Leave You by H. E. Francis, selected by Diane Glancy

The Logic of a Rose: Chicago Stories by Billy Lombardo, selected by Gladys Swan

Necessary Lies by Kerry Neville Bakken, selected by Hilary Masters

Love Letters from a Fat Man by Naomi Benaron, selected by Stuart Dybek

Tea and Other Ayama Na Tales by Eleanor Bluestein, selected by Marly Swick

Dangerous Places by Perry Glasser, selected by Gary Gildner

Georgic by Mariko Nagai, selected by Jonis Agee

Living Arrangements by Laura Maylene Walter, selected by Robert Olen Butler

Garbage Night at the Opera by Valerie Fioravanti,
selected by Jacquelyn Mitchard

Boulevard Women by Lauren Cobb, selected by Kelly Cherry

Thorn by Evan Morgan Williams, selected by Al Young

King of the Gypsies by Lenore Myka, selected by Lorraine M. López

Heirlooms by Rachel Hall, selected by Marge Piercy

The Owl That Carries Us Away by Doug Ramspeck, selected by Billy Lombardo